THE DASHING TEST PILOT

JOHN THOMPSON

1. RAF SPRING MILLS

RAF Spring Mills lay sunbathing under the warm June sun. One of those rare perfect days in England when the bees buzzed, the birds twittered and the leaves rustled in the warm zephyrs.

RAF Spring Mills lay in Suffolk, just north of the Essex border but well away from the nearest town.

The airfield belonged to the Army following World War II, during which it had been part of Fighter Command protecting London. The Commanding Officer is a full General in the Army, Gen George Elliott who had been a leading light in the First and Second Gulf Wars as well as Kosovo. He now chose to head up this sleepy RAF facility. His assistant is the legendary Patricia Baynes ranked first among all the civil servants in the government, she could have any job she wanted but she chooses to remain at RAF Spring Mills. There are no other office staff as none are needed.

The entrance gate is manned by Corporal (Cpl) Joe Shaw, the "Hero of Helmond." During a vicious firefight several soldiers were trapped in a burning building and Joe rushed in and carried them out one by one under fire from the Taliban. Joe got everyone out but was hit several times and as a result lost his left hand and right leg below the knee. He received England's highest honor, the Victoria Cross given for gallantry above and beyond the call of duty. Many months of medical procedures followed but Joe made a full recovery using an artificial hand and artificial leg. He could not return to combat duties but was offered the post at RAF Spring Mills which he accepted but turned down the rank of Sergeant.

THE DASHING TEST PILOT BY JOHN THOMPSON

The other staff on the base consisted of a small medic team, catering, cleaning and repairs. These people were all locals and were treated as civilians but were paid by the army.

Why then is RAF Spring Mills nicknamed "England's Area 51?" It has no aliens, there are no UFOs hidden away and it does not retro-engineer alien craft, nor indeed does it develop top secret aircraft.

The reason is because of the operations carried out there. From Monday through Thursday it is a training base for special forces; The Special Air Service (SAS) who carry out covert operations, counter-terrorism, direct action and hostage rescue; The Special Boat Service (SBS) who are also counter-terrorists but using daring undercover raids; MI5 who are the domestic counter-intelligence and security agency; and MI6 who are the foreign intelligence service collecting, analyzing and taking action in behalf of national security. The training is mainly carried out in a vast underground facility beneath the base which houses firing ranges, unarmed combat areas, espionage equipment and other things I am not supposed to know about. Physical training, which the public sometimes glimpse is carried out on a section of the airfield away from the runway.

On Friday the SAS and others guard the perimeter with orders to use deadly force if necessary. Friday is the day the test pilot operates. It is not often new top secret military aircraft are tested, mostly it is aircraft that have had a fault repaired or a part replaced and the aircraft has to be put through its paces to make sure the aircraft will be fully operational. Civil as well as military aircraft pass through, mostly the flying is routine. However, on rare occasions an ancient aircraft is needed to be tested for an air show. The locals have been treated to the sight and sound of Spitfires, Hurricanes, Mosquitoes, Typhoons, Lancasters, and once a Sopwith Camel that had been specially constructed for a First World War picture.

I hear you ask, "Who is the test pilot?"

He is none other than the legendary Colonel (Col) John Thompson [**AUTHOR'S NOTE** A little poetic license here. He has my name and character but I can't fly for toffee nor am I heroic except in the mirror.] Col Thompson served in Kosovo, Iraq and Afghanistan but was considered too valuable to be lost to the RAF in combat and was transferred to RAF Spring Mills as test pilot and was soon dubbed "The Dashing Test Pilot" by the press. His exploits and near misses with disaster were lapped up by the public and even by members of the Cabinet, we all need our heroes after all. He was sometimes called "Biggles" by the tabloids but Col Thompson soon put a stop to that in view of copyright issues with the Estate of Capt W E Johns the creator of Biggles. [**AUTHOR'S NOTE** For the record I still read Biggles Books and also Just William, Sexton Blake and Sherlock Holmes. My literary tastes are the nazz]

This information that has gone before raises the question, "Why is it England's Area 51?" Again it was the press, as they are never allowed in while the SAS and others are there nor on the rare times that a secret military aircraft is being tested, plus, the notices about the use of deadly force that are strategically placed around the perimeter fence. Indeed, everyone who works or trains at RAF Spring Mills has to sign and be bound by the Official

Secrets Act. Try as they may, and believe me they have really tried, RAF Spring Mills does not reach the heights of conspiracy that is the hallmark of Area 51.

On Thursday the ground crew for the testing is brought in from RAF Lakensham, which is nearby, to assist Col Thompson in preparing the aircraft for testing. The ground crew judiciously ignore the shenanigans of MI6 and others but they do eat with them at lunchtimes where the subjects discussed range from football (Ipswich Town and Arsenal), rugby (Leeds Rhinos-my team had to mention them), Cricket (Essex) and politics (never discussed).

This peace was suddenly disturbed by the sound of a police siren coming towards the main gate. …

2. A RUDE POLICEMAN

The police car skidded to a halt and the front seat passenger got out. He was a tall, dark haired man in his late twenties wearing the sort of clothes CID officers wore in the sixties. He carried a very angry expression on his face.

He looked at Cpl Shaw and screamed, "You, my man, come here now you are in the presence of a superior officer and should do as you are told." He pointed at the ground just in front of himself and shouted, "Here, now, you oik, you have two seconds to get here you common pleb, if you don't your career is over."

Joe Shaw just looked at him stolidly almost without blinking and certainly not making any movement.

The police officer continued to rant. "If this was wartime you would be shot for disobedience. You lower ranks should know your place … for the last time come here."

Joe remained unmoving and unmovable.

The rear seat passenger exited the police car, moved towards the police officer, grabbed him by the lapels and slammed him against the guard hut. This man was very tall and muscular with the most menacing skinhead haircut.

He said to the police officer, who was trembling with fear, "I know 169 ways to kill you without using a weapon and I know how to dispose of bodies; believe me I've done it so many times, so killing lowlife scum like you and getting rid of your unworthy carcass will be no more difficult than changing my socks. Wanna die scuzzer?"

Joe remained expressionless.

The big man went on. "The man you have talked down to and insulted is Cpl Joe Shaw, the greatest hero the British Army has had in recent years. He is "the hero of Helmond," ring any bells?"

The police officer, whose name is Phil Jackson, said, "I am so sorry Cpl, I didn't know who you were. We would like to see Gen Elliott please, we have been sent by the Foreign Secretary, Boris Johnson. Here is my warrant card."

Joe looked at the warrant card which identified Phil as Detective Chief Inspector (DCI) Philip Jackson of the Met. [**AUTHOR'S NOTE** The Met is the common term for The Metropolitan Police Force based at New Scotland Yard in London with 180 police stations and over 32,000 staff]. He went back into the hut. The hut was fixed with state of the art cameras and sound equipment which had to be patched through to the General's office at all times for obvious security reasons.

Joe said to Gen Elliott, "Did you hear and see that sir?"

"I did, Joe, the Old Bill have got a rude one there. Can you find out who the other guy is please and why they want to see me?"

Joe opened the door and said, "Who are you sir (to the large man) and why do you want to see the general? (to Phil)"

The large man said "I am MI6 guarding this weasel in case he gets into trouble. I have failed, so I will beat him up later. I have no ID and we do not reveal our names so that if you were interrogated by the enemy you could truthfully say you don't know."

Phil said, "It is a matter of national security so we would appreciate your letting us in Cpl Shaw and again I apologize for being rude to you."

A voice from the hut said, "Fine, Joe, do let them in and their driver can have a meal on us in the canteen, They are aware."

Joe opened the gate and pointed where to park, he also told the police driver, Sergeant (Sgt) Peter Simpson to go for a meal in the canteen. They parked the police car outside the general's office and walked in.

Patricia Baynes sat demurely at her desk and as the two walked in she said, "Good morning, how may I help?"

Phil went off on one again. "You must stand when a superior officer enters the room, it is bad manners to remain seated in my presence, you should know your place. Did they not teach you this in the army? This place is a disgrace, no discipline. I am going to report it to the MoD (Ministry of Defense)."

Patricia looked at him and said, "Finished have we? I will tell the general you are here."

A voice came over the intercom. "I heard all that Patricia send them in."

Phil and the man with no name came in and sat down.

Gen Elliott said, "A disgrace eh? You jumped up little toad. You are a DCI, I am a General I outrank you pal. I am not prepared to let this go."

He pressed a few keys on his console and there appeared on two large screens Boris Johnson the Foreign Secretary and Phillip Hammond the Defense Secretary."

Boris said, "Hi, George. We will send a car for you Sunday to come to the cricket. If we win it's the Championship for Essex and even Phillip is coming as a glory supporter."

Gen Elliott explained in a few words what had happened.

Boris looked angry and snarled, "Phil Jackson, you are not a copper, you are a travel clerk and to think I trusted you to do this job. You have insulted a great hero, the best civil servant in the world and the best general in the army. Who do you think you are?"

Before Phil could reply Phillip Hammond said, "Do you know what the penalty is for impersonating a police officer? It is 6 months in jail- shall we arrest you?"

Phil replied, "I did it so we could see the General quicker. I was taught to remind people that they should know their place from my history teacher at school and I firmly believe he was right. I am sorry for my rudeness but I feel I should stick to my principles here." …

3. WHY PEOPLE SHOULD KNOW THEIR PLACE

Boris said, "Let me explain folks, When the socialists were in charge that old class warrior Gordon Brown said we must not ask applicants for the senior civil service where they went to school as we could be accused of elitism if we stuffed our ranks with public school attenders to the exclusion of all others. I agree and I know Philip Hammond does also as it applies to the MoD. So Phil Jackson you have never been asked about your educational background. Let us start at the end, you have a degree in IT and politics so I presume you went to a decent uni. Which one, pray do tell?"

Phil replied, "Christ Church. My dad is very wealthy so he could send me there. It gives the best education of any uni."

Boris continued, "And there did they teach you inveterate snobbery, you know, that everyone should know their place?"

"No they are very egalitarian, any rank there you have to work jolly hard for and need to be humble."

Boris then said, "So, Phil, where did you go to school?"

"Eton College."

Boris smiled and said kindly, "That is my alma mater too, but I was never taught to tell people they should know their place. If I did it here at the Foreign Office the trade union would be on my back. You do it and they do not seem to bother."

Phil replied, "I am a member of the executive committee and so they let it go."

Boris said, "I have had some of the junior members coming to me to complain about you but I have never got round to doing anything about it, *mea culpa.* When you come back, unless you apologize to the General, Joe Shaw and the lovely Patricia, you will be fired, got that?"

Phil said, "I will formally apologize before we leave, I promise on my honour."

Boris continued, "So how come Eton taught you that horrendous expression? I went there, Philip Hammond also, the General and Col Thompson, the dashing test pilot, went there as well. Mr MI6 with no name where did you go, or is that an Official Secret too?"

The MI6 agent replied, "Call me Colin, it's not my name but it will do, I went to the Ian Mikardo School in Mile End then to Imperial College. I think we are all equal."

Phil had had time to gather his thoughts and went on to say. "Our history master, who I had throughout at Eton, instilled those principles of social hierarchy in me. He must have said 'The lower classes should know their place and defer to those of us who are their superiors.' in every single lesson. His name was Braithwaite Shunk D'Eem and in my view he was a brilliant historian. One could not fault his knowledge or teaching ability, and he was a thoroughly nice chap."

Phillip Hammond said, "I had him one year but as I am much older than you, I can tell you he was different in my day. Yes, he was brilliant and very nice but he never mentioned the phrase I will not repeat. In later years, he developed Alzheimer's hence some of what he said came from what he had learned, you know, Oscar Wilde, Mrs Gaskell etc. The governors monitored his progress and for years decided that his occasional lapses were harmless. Nobody took much notice of them, erm, apart from one, you Phil. Did you not realize he was losing it and that some of his words were out of their time, the guy was an anachronism albeit a lovely one."

Boris said, "Do your apologies then we can get down to business."

Phil quickly apologized to Joe, Patricia and the General, then came back and sat down.

Patricia sent for Col John Thompson who appeared quickly. He looked at the monitors and said, "Wow, political royalty. Hi guys and you are here because..?"

Boris said, "We have a little job for you, o dashing test pilot. It involves a week's worth of work in a certain foreign country testing a new hush hush military aircraft. You will be accompanied by the two people you do not know in that room. Phil Jackson is an amazing computer nerd who will help you from ground control and Colin, that is not his name but you may call him thus, who is from MI6 and can drive any vehicle of any size plus will act as protection. You will be paid by us, we will provide all expenses plus at the end of the mission you will receive a bonus from the foreign power with tax deducted which you will get back at the end of their tax year. You only need to take underwear and personal items as all uniforms etc will be issued by the foreign power who have all your measurements. Are you good with that, John?"

Col Thompson's handsome face wore a slight frown. "Where are we going?"

Boris said, "Peter Simpson our driver will bring you back here. I can't tell you over Skype as it can be hacked."

Col Thompson said, 'Very well then I agree. However, there is something I want from Mr

Hammond which has been bothering me for a while. Cpl Joe Shaw should be a Sergeant (Sgt) and should work for me as I am a test pilot but I get a shed load of paperwork to do after each mission. Promote him, give him to me and backdate his promotion five years so he gets a decent lump sum, is that in order Mr Hammond?"

Philip replied, "Absolutely, John. Get Patricia to draw up the papers and I will send a police car for them."

Patricia's voice came over the intercom. "I've done them Mr Hammond all enveloped up. I suggest you ring Chelmsford Police and ask for Inspector Moore. He will collect the papers for you."

With that and goodbyes the party headed for the car park for the journey to the Foreign Office. …

4. CAN I PRESS THE SIREN?

Sgt Peter Simpson was waiting for them in the car park, they quickly got in. Col Thompson sat in the front.

They stopped at the front gate so Phil could apologize to Cpl Shaw. After a brief discussion they hugged and Phil resumed his seat. All seemed peaceful as they drove through the Suffolk countryside.

Col Thompson smiled shyly and said to Sgt Simpson, "Pete, is this a real police car?"

"Yes at the FO we have two police cars driven by me and Sgt Joseph Turner. We get involved in serious crimes such as terrorism or bank robberies but they are only in emergencies. Our main job is to pick certain VIPs up at the airport and bring them to Mr Johnson or the Prime Minister. This is for ones who are seen as possible terrorist or assassination targets and who do not have sufficient security of their own. We are accompanied by an armed officer either from MI5 or the Royal Protection Squad. I cannot say anymore."

Col Thompson replied, "I did not know that. How long have you been doing the job?"

"I was five years with the Sweeney [**AUTHOR'S NOTE** The Sweeney is a nickname for a branch of the Met Serious Crime Squad who investigate robberies. Sweeney comes from Cockney rhyming slang "Sweeney Todd"=Flying Squad. The officers are armed with Glock 17 pistols and have been very successful over the years.] and then I transferred to the FO twenty years ago."

Col Thompson said, "Do you still keep all the authority you had at the Sweeney?"

"Yes, I have powers of arrest and charging which Joseph and I used in Operation Lockup where we were added to police strength for a day in lightning raids on terrorists in the East End a couple of years ago. We cleaned up a lot of nasties that day."

"So, how is it you are taking me to the FO with my backpack of personals? I could have got the train from Ipswich and the tube to the FO?"

"Orders from on high Colonel, I think you are a precious cargo for this mission. I gather it is not routine or, as you say, you could have got the train. But ours is not to reason why, eh?"

"Quite right Peter. On a slightly different subject, since I was a little boy growing up in Leeds I have always wanted to play the siren on a police car. Would that be ok or is it against regulations?"

"It is against regulations but we are on a mission so if Colin and DCI Phil don't mind..."

Colin said, "Fine."

Phil said, "Ok but don't call me DCI I got in trouble from Boris for that."

Col Thompson pressed the button on the dash and the siren began its "NEE NAAH" much to the Colonel's delight. They proceeded on their merry way when they came upon two cars parked. Three men with guns appeared to be threatening a man and a woman.

The police car screeched to a halt and the four got out. The three armed men panicked and headed into the woods.

Peter said, "Phil find out what happened. Colin and John let's get 'em."

They set off in pursuit and as all three men were fit they soon caught up to the three runaways.

One of the bad men reached for his gun but Colin dived at him knocking the wind out of his sails. He picked him up by the throat and grabbed his arm in a brutal arm lock that caused the guy to scream, "You're breaking my arm." "Correct." said Colin and there was a snap of bone which set the guy screaming again.

Peter caught his man by the collar and rammed his face into the ground. The guy said, Please don't hurt me." Peter said, "You were going to shoot someone so eat this." Peter gave him a savage kidney punch.

The man John was chasing threw down his gun and went for John. John had trained with the SAS at RAF Spring Mills and so could fight. He hit the guy with a full forearm breaking his nose then a heart punch that felled him.

The three heroes took the villains back to the car. Several police cars were waiting with DCI Moore of Chelmsford Police.

He said, "I was on my way from RAF Spring Mills after picking up a package from Patricia at the behest of the Defense Secretary so I called for back up when Phil here, gave me the shout. We have been after these scrotes for two years. They act like Dick Turpin, they pretend to have had an accident and when a car stops they rob the passengers at gunpoint and usually steal the car as well. They've not killed anyone yet and so they will not get life but ten years in a Cat A prison might sort them out. Thank you so much."

Col Thompson explained, "So as they had not killed yet, that would explain why the scrote I tackled threw his gun away. He thought he could beat me in a fair fight but he couldn't."

DCI Moore said to Colin, "The one you tackled wants to bring an assault charge against you. It won't stick though."

Colin went up to the villain and said, "Bring your charge mate. I am with MI6 we know how to remove people permanently." He shoved his face right into the villains face and snarled, "Tired of living sunshine?"

The villain began to sob, "Please don't kill me I won't press charges I promise."

"You won't or it will be a slow agonizing death for you sunshine."

DCI Moore said, 'Thanks again lads. As you are on a secret mission, credit for this goes to us. So good luck with things and let's cheer Essex on to the Championship."

Our four heroes continued their drive to the FO with the siren blaring. …

5. A MEETING WITH BORIS

They arrived at the Foreign Office with no further holdups either with guns or traffic, mainly due to excessive use of the siren. It was all bells and whistles flying up Whitechapel Road as if they were chasing bandits. Thankfully, there were no accidents or scattered pedestrians. Peter enjoyed the driving; Colin could not care less; John was like a kid in a toy shop with sparkling eyes and a grin stretching the length of Whitechapel Road; and Phil was a little queasy as he preferred a sedentary life.

They parked in the VIP car park at the back of the FO. They were all four admitted on Peter's pass and ushered into Boris's office.

"Gentlemen," Boris boomed, "welcome have a pew."

He reached for his intercom button and said, "Charlotte my sweet, please bring in five lovely coffees and a giant plate of choccie biccies."

"At once, Boris." said Charlotte Pinkney-Brabazon, who was Boris's secretary and, despite the name, was very efficient as well as being very attractive.

"So then, my heroes, you have brought much credit to the FO with your handling of the villains especially the necessary rough stuff. There is too much molly coddling of villains these days, if all the police were like you four we would have less villainy and less fear throughout the country. Sadly, as you are on a secret mission you will get no credit except from me. The guy whose arm Colin broke is not pressing charges, he says it was an accident but I think you may have mentioned MI6 and the liquidation of troublesome people, am I correct, Colin?"

"Indeed you are, sir, I might have just slipped the odd word in his ear but he understood. My secret is safe."

Boris turned to Peter. "I would imagine, Peter, you are wondering why you are in this meeting, especially as we are not dealing with the picking up of VIPs. Well, I know you go on holiday after you have completed this mission and it has been a tough time for you since Avril died and so to help I have decided, as Foreign Secretary, to allow you to use the police car for your holiday and also here is a Foreign Office debit card I would like you to use to pay for stuff on your holiday. The FO will pick up the tab, it has been approved by the Prime Minister and Home Secretary at a Cabinet meeting so have no fear of using it. You can sit in on the rest of the meeting which will be brief and then you can take the lads to Heathrow."

Peter teared up, "I don't know what to say, sir, you are too kind."

Boris grinned, "It is the rare caring face of government Peter. You have done sterling service for us over the years ferrying unpleasant people here and taking part in anti-terrorist work along with Joseph. You deserve it, buddy."

Charlotte brought in the coffee and biscuits on a legendary government tea trolley. She distributed the mugs of coffee and chocolate digestives to everyone.

She said to Phil Jackson, "Thank you for the e-mail Phil, apology accepted."

She left after smiling perfectly at everyone. Phil blushed to his roots as he, like everyone who ever met her, was madly in love with Charlotte.

Boris said, "Charlotte Pinkney-Brabazon is our secret weapon, she is a one woman charm offensive and is not one of these idle rich debutante types, she is from an ordinary home but is blessed with incredible looks and talent. However, gentlemen, down to business."

The four looked expectantly at Boris who now had a kind of puzzled look on his face.

"The Yanks want to borrow you, dashing test pilot, to test fly a prototype hush hush aircraft, which is apparently equipped with oodles of top secret spying equipment like cameras and other gubbins. They will pay the three of you for the mission. You will be taxed in the USA but will get the tax back at the end of the year. They will describe the job as test flying a repaired civil airliner. I asked the Chief of Staff of the Americans why they did not use their own test pilots as they were more than capable. He said that it was in case the aircraft was a duff one or the equipment did not work. They believe we are better at keeping secrets, which we bally well are. You will fly commercial from Heathrow using the VIP entrance where Peter will drop you and you will be business class so there will be more leg room and British Airways is the best airline to fly. The press should not be there, but when you arrive in Las Vegas, if any of the press try to do an interview, simply tell them you are on holiday with your two assistants and you are very tired after a long flight so need your bed. You will be met by General Buck Wade who will be your CO for the duration which will only be a week or two. He will personally fly you to, wait for it, Area 51 which will be your base.

Apparently, your section is the most secret part of Area 51 so you may get to meet some aliens, who knows? Phil is going with you, despite the problems coming from him, as your wingman on the electronics side, Phil is one of the world experts in IT so will keep you safe electronically. Colin is going as HGV (Heavy Goods Vehicle) driver for the vehicle which will carry the craft and also as muscle in case of any trouble. We hope the mission can be done in less than two weeks. Your report you will dictate for it to be typed up. When you get back newly appointed Sgt Joe Shaw will be your new assistant and as I understand from George he is a first class secretary. Right then, guys, off you go and have fun. …

6. HEATHROW

The drive to Heathrow Airport was uneventful, they used the A40, A4 and M4 and arrived at the VIP entrance in good time. There was some judicious use of the siren again but only occasionally to pass small clumps of traffic on the M4. Heathrow looked its usual busy self with people scurrying about like ants on a mission. Everyone seemed to look anxious except for the dashing test pilot and party.

Peter drove them to the VIP entrance and after saying their farewells and the old English custom of wishing Peter a lovely holiday they grabbed their luggage and entered the VIP lounge. The official on the door checked their tickets and directed them to the dining area.

Phil said, "I checked out this VIP lounge. All food and drink is free as part of the fare so we can have what we want. According to the inveterate traveler's guide, however, it is suggested that you do not eat much if traveling by British Airways as they feed you copious amounts of food , which is top quality.

John said, "What do you suggest we have then Phil?"

"Coffee and donuts. The Boston Cream Donut, it is a round donut topped with chocolate icing and filled with a creamy custard filling."

Colin said, "Let's go for it, Phil."

Phil ordered three white coffees and three Boston Cream Donuts, which arrived in double quick time. [**AUTHOR'S NOTE** In the interest of research I had to try the Boston Cream Donut in a well known establishment and they are delicious. Other types of donut are available.]

Colin said very quietly, "Do not mention our mission at all as three tables away is an old acquaintance from the Chinese Embassy who would be interested t know where we are going especially with someone as famous as you John."

The three nodded and Phil said loudly, "I am a dyed in the wool Chelsea fan, how about you guys?"

Colin said, "I'm a regular on the Millwall terraces looking for a great season and promotion, what about you John?"

John's reply was different, "I'm not really a football fan, when I go back to Leeds for a visit with rellies I watch Leeds Rhinos rugby league team, they are excellent."

Phil said, "We once had a bit of an office trip to watch the London Broncos play Dewsbury Rams. A very entertaining game I must admit but the tackling seemed brutal."

John said, "It does look bad to an outsider but these guys train day in and day out so they are among the fittest sportsmen around and they are conditioned to take hard knocks."

Colin meanwhile walked over to the Chinese Embassy official and greeted him cheerily. They both spoke Chinese for a while and then Colin returned to the other two.

He began, "Li Cho is going back to Beijing as he has been promoted to a role training future Chinese spies being sent to Russia, so it is of no interest to MI6. He was a great spy who had the respect of MI6 from top to tea lady. He was never a target as the Chinese did not use rough house tactics so we were always gentlemen with them. We had no military secrets they were interested in and in any event it would be difficult for the Chinese to infiltrate any of our top secret bases, we tended to use them in training camps as they are excellent teachers and an asset to our armed forces."

Colin continued, "So then, what other sports do we like, I'll go first. I love MMA and train with an MMA school in Barking to keep up the old fitness levels. I also like to watch tennis, a great tactical game, I like to work out each player's style, strengths and weaknesses. Phil?"

Phil replied, "Cricket, mainly for the statistics. I go watch Essex when I can and take my own score book. I can only usually get to the T20 matches which last a couple of hours and are most exciting, particularly as Essex are so good at the short game. Also I like to watch American Football which is an intricate game of tactics and formations plus oodles of statistics of all sorts. John?"

John thought for a moment and then said, "Cricket but Yorkshire not Essex purely because I was born there and it's compulsory to support them. I rarely go to games unless they play in Essex, Surrey or Middlesex. Sometimes I can get there if they play on a Monday or Tuesday. I like tennis as well for the reasons Colin gave."

Phil went to the bar for three more white coffees but no more donuts as they would eat on the plane. By this time Li Cho had departed for the Beijing flight which left no one sitting near our three heroes and so Colin spoke quietly once more.

"When we get on the plane, here is a tip from the dumb guide to the MI6- do not speak unless it is necessary and never, ever mention your mission. You see once a party of three start to talk their security starts to falter and it should be remembered that the guy behind you could be listening for you to betray your mission. I know it sounds a bit John Le Carre but as the old posters used to say 'walls have ears.' [**AUTHOR'S NOTE** this is an old World War II slogan that appeared on posters all over England, based on the premise that everyone might be a Nazi spy] I suggest we all just order our food and watch movies or binge watch *Downton Abbey* or something as we know where we are going and what John will be doing so we need only wait to be briefed by General Wade."...

7. INCIDENT IN THE AIRPORT

The VIP lounge major domo came across to the three and said, "You may board when you are ready gentlemen. Business class boards first, as you know, thirty minutes before the rest and as you are the only ones in business class today it would be good if you wouldn't mind boarding now so that we can board the rest without any last minute pushing and shoving."

Phil said, "That's fine, we will do as you ask. Gate 1 I believe which is just next to the entrance to this place, is this correct?"

The major domo replied, "Indeed it is, enjoy your flight, gentlemen."

The three headed for the door of the VIP lounge and as they went through the automatic doors they heard someone screaming in Chinese. It was a young man holding a gun on Li Cho.

Colin whispered, "The guy with the gun is from some kind of triad and is accusing Li Cho of trying to destroy the triad. Hold my bag while I help Li Cho."

Colin gently eased towards the young man from the rear and in one swift move chopped his wrist which caused him to drop the gun and then grabbed both arms in a chicken wing hold which was very painful. The young man knew enough to know that if he moved he would have severe damage to his joints.

Two plain clothes men pushed through the crowd and when they saw the scenario said "Well done, sir, you have saved a nasty international incident and the life of an important Chinese Embassy official."

Colin handed the young man over and whispered, "My pleasure MI5. Li Cho is a good friend of ours so deal with this miscreant harshly or hand him over to us."

   The MI 5 officer smiled and said, "MI6? We are keeping him as we are trying to break up triads over here at the request of the Chinese government as they cannot operate officially as crime busters in England and the Old Bill seem powerless, maybe some corruption at a high level. Do you want to make a statement?"

   "No, I'm flying somewhere departing soon, you guys take the credit. Also Li Cho is flying back to China now so he won't be making a statement either."

   The young Chinese man said, in English, "We will hunt you down and kill you for the great insult you have made to the Blue Boar Triad."

   Colin got right in the face of the Chinese man and said, "Bring it Dolly Daydream, you take on MI6 at your peril. We don't use the courts we administer justice the old fashioned way, your bunch of criminals without honor will crumble into dust before we have finished. Mark my words, dragon breath."

   The MI5 men, who were acting as security in the area at the request of Phillip Hammond, took the young man away to MI5 HQ to be questioned in the unlikely hope of his betraying his triad team mates. Because the mission of Col Thompson was so important to the Americans, MI5 were to be on duty as security in addition to the normal Heathrow Security Force. It was the usual spooks Hammond was worried about, not criminal gangs and so whilst one menace was dealt with, there still remained the spook threat. In fact in the crowd was a member of the FSB whose sole job was to see which flight the intrepid trio took so they could scramble a small team as a welcoming party for Col Thompson, when he arrives at his destination. He, Yuri Grodny, for that was his name, had his phone in his hand and an inane grin on his face. He was taking random shots of the ceiling, the departure desks and the

other hardware of a busy international airport. He had seen what had happened and took a brief video of Colin, Phil and John, then he waited for further developments.

Yuri kept close behind the three as they threaded their way towards Departure Gate One. He heard the Flight Announcement for Business Class Boarding for Las Vegas and wondered why they were Heading for Las Vegas, why not Washington DC or Los Angeles. He also was questioning why the dashing test pilot had with him a minor official from the Foreign Office, who was not on the FSB radar, and a trained killer from MI6, who was seen as a major threat to FSB as a couple of years ago the MI6 man had taken down a crack FSB team of assassins who were after the British Ambassador to New Zealand, he had killed all three in a fire fight. Yes, the FSB feared Colin but they knew if they murdered him then the full might of MI6 would be brought to bear which would sound the death knell of the FSB and possibly also, MI6 might start picking off Russian politicians. The orders from the Kremlin were to steer well away from Colin, only maintain a low level watching brief, as Colin and others were excellent at removing terrorists permanently and no longer viewed Russia as the enemy, which had been the case for decades in the Cold War. Yuri used his phone to text the Russian Embassy FSB chief with a short message which read, "Dasher going to Las Vegas. May change there. Have gazelle ready."

The message, which was sent in a cryptic code, would be relayed to Mikhael Sverdski the Station Head in America, literally the face of FSB, who would send a small team to Las Vegas to monitor events, but not to interfere unless Russia was threatened. Spying was not as exciting as it used to be but Yuri and others made the best of a boring job which was well paid for just being eavesdroppers with very little action, unlike MI6 who still acted as a bunch of James Bonds [**AUTHOR'S NOTE** James

Bond is a super-spy created by Ian Fleming in the 1950s and still popular today through a series of movies.] The three were at the Departure gate ready to fly. …

8. FLYING DOWN TO VEGAS

The team were safely ensconced in their opulent business class seats ready for the off, waiting for the economy class to squeeze into their seats, although it must be said that there is more room on British Airways flights than on most other airlines. Although they did not know of FSB interest in their flight, Colin did suspect that they would be met by an FSB team for surveillance purposes. The FSB would not make contact, just follow them and presumably be deterred by Area 51 security which was probably the tightest of the tight.

Phil grinned and said, "Colin, are you going to watch a spy film during the flight?"

Colin replied, "No, mate, I thought I'd watch a few episodes of *Doctor Who* Season 12 as I missed it. Love the adventures of the good doctor, me. Why what are you going to watch Phil, *Yes Minister?* Right up your alley I'd have thought."

Phil retorted, "I am going to watch any replays of Chelsea's matches they have, failing that one or more *Batman* films, I quite see my self as the Caped Crusader but I can't fight for toffee. What about you John, what are you going to watch?"

John smiled and said, "Anything Leeds Rhinos related but if not then one of the old English detective series, I dunno, maybe *Morse, Poirot, DCI Banks* something on those lines."

Colin went on, "The food is meant to be ace so tuck in and enjoy. We will meet the tour guide in Vegas who will show us to our hotel and tell us what would be some good things to do. So, when they've done the emergency procedures bit we can relax for the next dozen or so hours.

THE DASHING TEST PILOT BY JOHN THOMPSON

The flight was uneventful, the team said little as Colin had earlier advised. The food was magnificent and eventually all three dozed off being supplied with pillows and blankets by the attentive cabin crew,

whose sole aim was to look after the comfort and safety of all the passengers but especially business class. There were no panic attacks, drunken incidents or medical emergencies and so the flight went smoothly and by the numbers.

The plane landed smoothly at McCarran International Airport which is about five miles south of Las Vegas Downtown area. Business class deplanes first so our heroes left the plane smoothly with no pushing and shoving which is often the case with economy class passengers but usually only on holiday flights to Spain. They walked and rode through several corridors until reaching customs. All three went through smoothly without a hitch as they were of course VIP passengers.

They reached the luggage reclaim section there to be met by a huge man wearing combat fatigues but no insignia apart from a small patch that said "Wade"

He approached them, shook hands and said, "Hi, I'm Buck Wade, let's get this show on the road."

Suddenly, Colin darted off and brought back a small man, holding him in a painful looking armlock.

Colin said, "Why are you here, *druzhishche?* Tell me or I'll break your arm."

The Russian FSB agent, named Leo Grebski, said, "Our Embassy in Washington asked me to monitor you. This is not the Cold War so you do not need to use force, I am not muscle just watcher. We mean you no harm we know you are a dangerous killer. Let me go and I promise we will not follow you. You are going to Area 51 as you have the famous Dashing Test Pilot with you. We are interested in the plane he is testing as we have no information on it."

Just then three CIA goons arrived. "Hey, how ya doin' General? Want us to take this lowlife away and shoot him."

Colin looked at them and shook his head. "He's just an observer, treat him well, hold him for a few hours then ring the Russian consulate in Vegas to come and get him and next time to use someone with a bit more skill."

General Buck Wade had gaped open mouthed at the events and said, "Wow! Here I am thinking this is just a routine test flight and I'm in the middle of a spy movie. Exciting times. Now, I will drive you to a secluded part of McCarran where we get aboard a plane run by Janet airline that will take us to Area 51. It is a 40 minute flight and is very secure indeed. I only have one pass so it should cover all four of us."

They arrived at the small terminal Janet used and went to the gate. However, as the three Englishmen did not have passes Sergeant (Sgt) Gonzalez refused them permission to board. Buck took out his phone, put someone on the screen and handed the phone to Sgt Gonzalez, who, after a brief conversation said, "Yes, sir, I will, sir and it is an honor to serve you and my country."

He looked at General Wade, saluted him again and said, "That was the Chief of Staff at the White House. He said passes were unnecessary for our three visitors and so I say welcome friends, please board the plane."

General Wade patted Sgt Gonzalez on the shoulder and said, "You are doing a fine job sergeant, you are a credit to your unit and the US Army"

Sgt Gonzalez beamed as the party of four boarded the plane with their rucksacks which of course were not searched. They settled down for the short flight over the desert to the legend that is Area 51.

Buck said, "When we get to our section I will give you a short briefing then time for sleep." …

9. THE TASK AHEAD

The flight took forty uneventful minutes and they landed on a huge runway and taxied up to what looked like a rundown airport lounge in some back of beyond country. Appearances can be deceptive and once past the deliberately distressed area of the entrance they were in a modern space-age air-conditioned lounge. A young lady in white scientific overalls approached them and said cheerfully, "Hi Buck, introduce me please."

Buck made the introductions and went on to say, "This lovely young lady is Kimberly Poeppy our scientific whizz. When she graduated from MIT [**AUTHOR'S NOTE** MIT is the Massachusetts Institute of Technology in Cambridge, Mass which has the reputation of being the top scientific learning institute in the world] with the highest marks ever, we were able to recruit her in the face of fearsome competition from many leading aerospace companies. She is treated with care."

Kim had a lovely warm smile which beamed out at our heroes. She said that she had been briefed on the three and these were her conclusions.

"Col. John Thompson known universally as The Dashing Test Pilot is the finest pilot ever with an impeccable record in combat and known for testing new European and Asian planes by putting them through vigorous testing scenarios, and is a fan of Leeds Rhinos, whoever they are. Philip Jackson works for the Foreign Office as a travel organizer but should be working in computers as he is able to think like a computer to solve problems in a logical manner. An unknown man I have to call Colin is a hitman from MI6 but is also able to drive any vehicle very quickly and safely."

The three nodded appreciatively.

Buck Wade said, "Kim looks after the scientific side of our work in that she can examine craft after and before the flight and can instantly solve problems without looking in manuals or consulting the

Internet. I just pick up a monthly check for sitting around while Kim does the work. We will go to our bit of the field now in our SUV."

Colin drove them and they were soon at a vast hangar away from most of the buildings but in sight of another vast hangar. They drove in the huge doors which had an armed guard waiting for them.

Buck sent the two soldiers away in their jeep and said "Don't move as this place transforms at the press of a button."

He took what looked like a small phone out of his pocket and pressed four numbers one after the other. The lights came on, a partition rolled up to the roof exposing a bank of computers and a fully equipped metallurgical laboratory and a small kitchen.

Kim said, "You guys will love the next bit."

Buck took a further small device from his pocket and pressed a button. There appeared a massive low-loader rig as if from nowhere with four metal tentacles snaking upwards being attached to something above the bed of the low-loader yet invisible. Kim climbed carefully onto the bed of the low-loader, she took what looked like a credit card from her pocket and inserted into a slot that had suddenly lit up in a rather fetching shade of blue. An invisible door moved outward toward her right and she disappeared from view. After a few seconds the entire craft suddenly appeared. It looked like a large

UFO [**AUTHOR'S NOTE** Unidentified Flying Object much beloved of science fiction writers going right back to H G Wells] but it had clearly been manufactured by humans. It had no military insignia on it nor maker's logo.

Kim said from the interior, "Come in and admire guys. John you will be flying this on a test flight of one day and depending on your report it will enter service in the USAF as a spy plane."

They all clambered aboard and noticed that there were not too many controls. No joystick but what appeared to be a games controller, there were several digital readers of altitude, speed et al as in normal aircraft and to the right were several small video screens but these were only lit white like a computer screen downloading.

Buck said, "Your mission, John, is to fly over several designated targets which you will photograph or film using the specially designed penetrating radar cameras which can film through concrete or down to the sea bed but while you are filming the screens will remain white as the info you bring back is top secret. You were told that American test pilots were afraid to fly this thing, it was a lie, you are the only one we can trust to keep a secret as we believe the FSB and Chinese Secret Service have infiltrated us, so we dare not use our own pilots. You will have no problem flying the craft as you could fly a broomstick and you will have back up from us on the ground. There is no communication device on board but Kim has reverse engineered this cheap watch to be a functioning radio and it also has some emergency features that we may not have to use. If

you get into any sort of trouble during the flight
press the button and you will be through to one of us.
The craft has no defensive armament but as you saw
it can be cloaked so it is invisible on radar, to
satellites and observers on the ground whether they
are using binoculars, heat profiling or night vision.
While you are inside the craft you will be invisible
too but you will be able to see out of the front screen.
Right then, we will cloak the craft and truck until
tomorrow. We will go eat in the officer's mess then
get a good night's sleep. The mission is tomorrow,
Wednesday, so you will be able to go back to
England on Friday. Thursday you can look at what
you have filmed, as can we."

The craft and low loader were both cloaked and
they headed off to the officer's mess. ...

10. CANTEEN SCRAP

In the officer's mess, the five all picked up the same "today's special" which was chicken pot pie with mashed potatoes and green beans. They also had hot chocolate and no dessert as they would be up with the lark in the morning. As they ate small talk was the order of the day, swapping tales of the desert with those of rural, sleepy Suffolk.

Six lower ranked officers walked in which made Colin reach for his phone and type in a password for the MI6 facial recognition app. He surreptitiously took a picture of the six and within a minute received back a reply. All six were known FSB operatives, Colin, who was sat next to General Wade, passed the phone to Gen. Wade and whispered, "Be prepared."

The largest of the FSB agents stood up and said in a perfect Illinois accent, "Hey guys, look it's the dashing test pilot we are all supposed to worship, the slimy Limey Col. John Thompson. He looks like a sack of manure that's gone right off. He looks like a yeller coward to me whose granmaw would whup his butt."

Gen. Wade said, "Stand down soldier, or I will put you on a charge. Show some respect for a senior officer."

The agent, Podnin, replied, "Get lost General, we are not in your outfit so you can't tell us what to do, if we want to insult this piece of English trash we will."

Colin chimed in, "Calm down Podnin or I'll arrest you."

Podnin sneered, "Who are you to threaten me, and my name is Sullivan not what you said."

Colin said, "All six of you are FSB working in a top secret US military installation. You are spies and as an MI6 operative I have a license to kill you. Do you want some, Podnin?"

Podnin screamed "*Atakovat ikh*" [**AUTHOR'S NOTE** Russian for "Attack them"] and all six leaped to their feet and went for John's party. The good guys also became vertical, ready to rumble. Let's unpack the fight which was over in seconds.

Philip Jackson learned to box and play rugby at Eton and so against his opponent he jumped at the guy's head and when he got him to the ground he laid him out with a combination of left and rights.

Gen. Wade had taken unarmed combat courses several times and so could handle himself well. He blocked a few wild swings by his Russian opponent before hitting him with a throat punch followed by a European elbow strike to the nose which rendered the Russian bloody and unconscious.

The dashing test pilot , who was not in the slightest bit angry about the Russian's insults grabbed his opponent by the lapels and in the style of Jamie Peacock [**AUTHOR'S NOTE** Jamie Peacock was a tremendous Leeds Rhinos player who was a very skillful rugby player but could also handle himself in a scrap] he applied a "Castleford Kiss" which is a savage head butt to the other guy's nose. The Russian's nose broke and John followed up with a back-handed chop across the throat that he had watched Ric Flair of WWE administer so often. This laid out his opponent.

Kim, whilst at MIT was women's champion at MMA for all four years of her attendance and was good enough to have turned professional. Her opponent laughed at her and called her "*Slabaya malenkaya devochka"* [**AUTHOR'S NOTE** Russian for "weak little girl"]. Kim knew what that meant and replied *"Polzat"* [**AUTHOR'S NOTE** Russian for "creep"] This annoyed the FSB thug who swung a vicious right at Kim's head, she swayed elegantly out of the way then kicked him on the knee, followed by a rapid succession of kicks to both hamstrings which brought him to his knees, she finished him with a devastating throat punch.

Colin grinned at his opponents, he said viciously, *"Vremya diya boli druz'ya"* [**AUTHOR'S NOTE** Russian for "time for pain friends"] The first one he knocked unconscious with an elbow strike to the temple. To Podnin he grinned evilly at and almost at light speed he grabbed his right arm in a strange looking lock and twisted. There were sickening tearing sounds from Podnin's elbow and shoulder. Colin dropped him to the floor where he writhed in pain until lapsing into unconsciousness.
[**AUTHOR'S NOTE** If this was a movie I think you would all be applauding our heroes so if any film producers would like to film this novella …]
Security had been called by the canteen manager and arrived promptly. After a few words from Gen. Wade the FSB agents were cuffed and dragged off to the brig.
Gen. Wade phoned the Pentagon and after many weird passwords and sequences of numbers was put through to the head of recruitment, Gen. Ditka.
Gen. Wade got straight to the point, "Mike, you guys have recruited six FSB agents to Area 51. My team and security have arrested them after a lovely struggle but you need to look into this, pronto, I

think you might have one of their guys in a high position, which could put US security at risk."

Gen. Ditka said, "We will do an immediate back check on them with CIA but we will come up with *Nada* as they are very clever at creating documents for people."

Gen. Wade said, "I have with me Colin from British MI6 who wants to talk to you."

Colin said, "General, here are some numbers and codes to ring to get through to our information gathering boffins. If these FSB scuzzers won't talk MI6 will lend you some of our finest who have so many painful ways to get info out of people."

The call ended there and the team calmly finished their tea. They returned in for bed after watching the movie *Fairfax Fights Fair Fact* ready for the big mission tomorrow. ...

11. DETAILS OF THE MISSION

The group breakfasted well at the canteen on bacon and scrambled eggs washed down with coffee then returned to their own little paradise in Area 51.

Gen. Wade had a single sheet of paper in his hand. He looked at it for a few moments and then began to speak.

"Your mission is twofold John, you are to test the flying and hovering ability of the craft and also this new type of camera which can take pictures through concrete and also water, especially sea water. You will only be flying over the US of A but all targets have been told when to expect you so they can see if they can pick you up. They will not fire missiles at you and have only been told that you will be flying and hovering over their bases. From what they can learn we hope to develop an anti-cloaking device here but as yet the Pentagon has not had a meeting to suggest budgeting for it. None of our potential enemies or friends have cloaking devices yet, but we believe Russia, China and you British are working towards one. Ours was developed by a Pentagon scientist. It basically blocks light reflected back from the craft, I don't know how but Kim has an idea how, when you are in flight she will give a copy of her notes to Philip who can pass them to your Ministry of Defense."

Gen. Wade went on after a slurp of coffee.

"You are to film five specific targets which are on this piece of paper but you will not be able to see the targets themselves, you will need to be on your best mettle to carry out pinpoint accuracy, but when you return we have permission to view what you have seen before it is transmitted to the Pentagon. If anything is revealed we will never mention it and in fact if it turns up nothing then that too will remain secret. The first target is here on Area 51, it is Hangar 7 and is supposed to be where the alien craft

from the Roswell crash in 1947 was held. The Pentagon says it is an empty hangar but we will look anyway. It is about five miles north east of here. When that one is finished you are to fly 435 miles east to Dulce in New Mexico. The mesa overlooking the town is believed to contain aliens on the seventh level underground but by filming from above we can watch the levels as we unpack each one."

Gen. Wade paused for a moment before continuing.

"From Dulce you will fly 831 miles south west to Santa Monica in California, fly around the bay filming it all as many people have seen UFOs rise from the depths and go back so many believe there is an undersea base below Santa Monica Bay. For mission number four we are not looking for UFOs but are doing a check on our radar security. For this you will fly 1,112 miles to Cheyenne Mountain in Colorado where you will fly at low level towards the entrance then fly up the mountain to see what we can see. From there you will fly due east 1,208 miles to Wright-Patterson Air Force Base in Ohio to make a movie of Hangar 18 which was the final resting place of the Roswell UFO, the Kecksberg UFO and a few others, all these missions are to check out conspiracy theories apart of course from Cheyenne Mountain which is to test out our defenses. The others were chosen as non-sensitive targets unlikely to produce results but will give the craft a good run out and will thoroughly test the new camera."

John asked, "How far is Wright-Patterson from here?"

Buck replied, "1,715 miles due east. It is a long trip but you can fly at Mach 3 which is 2,300 miles per hour so it would be a swift trip. Fly at a height of 40,000 feet to keep above commercial aircraft flight paths and for the filming come down to 500 feet. When you near your targets, which Kim has uploaded to your on-board computers, a buzzer will sound and you will need to decelerate to zero then descend at 150 mph until you reach optimum height. This is a tricky maneuver, which is why we have

chosen you. If the craft becomes operational with USAF it will take the place of satellites as it will be proof against being shot down. Here is the bad bit, as we said, there is no on-board communication device so if there is a problem you will have to use your watch which has a scrambler inbuilt so nobody can hear what you are saying. We would not be able to track you as obviously you are off the radar and so we will only know how you have done when you return and just say "back" into your radio. This is a prototype and so, without wanting to sound pessimistic, something may go wrong which is again why we have chosen you, John, as you are the best there is.

Kim said, "One of the worries with conventional aircraft is running out of fuel. This craft has a revolutionary engine that just uses energy particles taken in from its surroundings but it works and eliminates the need for dangerous fuel tanks. The course guidance system is excellent too as it will tell you where you are at the press of a button on a screen. Your targets are already input so you will just follow directions on the screens."

Phil said, "You can do it John, you are an even better pilot than Biggles."

John replied, "Wow! That is a real compliment indeed."

Buck said, "Right, are we ready to saddle up people?"

A resounding chorus of "heck, yeah!" and the mission began. …

12. TAKE OFF AND MISSION # ONE

The team went out ready for take off. John was wearing a one piece khaki suit to match with the desert should he have to make an emergency landing and also he knew to press the red button on the left arm rest of the pilot's seat to operate the safety belts which would hold him in if he had to make a crash landing.

John was aware that he would not be able to view the internal structures of objects he was filming using the penetration cameras as he had not signed the American equivalent of the Official Secrets Act. This did not concern him as he was a test pilot not a spook. The door was opened by a card which John wore around his neck on a ribbon. This was only for the prototype, any production model would have something more substantial. The craft was in cloaked mode as was the low loader. Colin operated the remote to unlock the driver's door and then pressed a further button to uncloak the low loader.

Kim and Phil were at the computer banks. Kim showed Phil the code to uncloak the craft remotely, which he did making the "flying saucer" appear miraculously. John swiped the card in the door opening slot and the door silently swung open. John boarded the craft and switched on the "electrics " ready for the off.

Colin shouted, "Shut the door John, so we can test your watch for sound."

Phil had his version of the watch in his hand and he pressed the left hand top button saying, "Can you 'ere me mother" [**AUTHOR'S NOTE** this was the catchphrase of Sandy Powell one of the many comedians I saw at the Leeds Empire theater when I was a young boy-nobody else remembers him which is sad but here he is memorialized in print].

John replied with "Who's on first?" [**AUTHOR'S NOTE** this is the name of a very funny sketch by Abbot and Costello that is found on You Tube and will make you chortle]

Phil replied "Loud and clear, Colin wants you to strap in while he drives out of the hangar onto the tarmac. Please confirm when it is done."

It took John a second to press the red button and be strapped in fully including his arms and legs. He said so the rest could hear him, "How am I supposed to fly it wrapped up like a fly in a spider's web?"

Buck replied, "The strapping is only for emergencies like a crash, the craft has an internal stabilizing mechanism so you do not need to be strapped in nor do you need to remain seated, you will be able to move around freely."

"OK! But it still seems a bit excessive."

Kim chipped in, "Straight after you are airborne just press the red button and you will be free of the strapping."

John replied, "That's fine but how do I takeoff when I'm trussed up like a chicken."

Kim replied, "We can do it remotely from here. We could have used it as a drone but in view of its purpose, apart from takeoff it is in the hands of the pilot. The effectiveness of the spidery web needed real time mission trials anyway, so if there is nothing else, off we go."

The low-loader was uncloaked as Colin swiftly and deftly reversed out of the hangar on to the tarmac. Once he was clear of the doors he cloaked the low-loader with the press of a button. The manufacturers of both the craft and low- loader both preferred a button that clicked so the driver/pilot would know the craft was cloaked.

Colin said into his microphone, "Ready to go."

Buck pressed the takeoff button and Colin felt the weight of the low loader lighten as the craft took off.

John felt the vertical thrust and immediately pressed the red button which released the safety webbing. He took the craft up to 40,000 feet then gently moving forward at 60 miles per hour he approached Hangar 7. Once over the target he hovered then slowly and gingerly descended to 500 feet above his target.

He pressed the camera button which began its filming, through concrete, of Hangar 7. John looked at the screen but it remained white. If the cameras were not working, that was not John's problem. He did note it responded to the controls brilliantly.

Back on the ground at Area 51 Colin reversed the low-loader into the hangar and dismounted.

"Job's a good 'un, smooth as butter with no hitches."

"Excellent, well done, Colin. Now we wait about twenty minutes before I contact the detection guys to see if anything registered. If it did we call him back in and abort the mission."

Phil said, "Do the three of us still get paid?"

Buck replied, "Of course, you are being paid by the USAF not some slimy toad in Washington."

To pass the time they watched the 24 hour news channel to keep an eye on the weather, especially for any tornado watches. There was an advisory for western Utah of possible tornadoes later in the day but it was only a possibility.

Colin said, "At 40,000 John should be flying over them, presumably the craft has been tested on a simulator for this kind of thing."

Kim said, "Actually, we don't know we can only presume it has but we can't be sure. He is the best pilot ever and so he should be able to handle it."

Colin said, "Typical of the military and aircraft manufacturers not doing a thorough job, so like the builders of the *Titanic*. Let's just hope for the best, eh?"

Buck said, "This project was done on a need to know basis due to all the foreign agents infiltrating. I have confidence that John can handle anything that comes at him."

"Let's hope so." said Colin....

13. TARGET #1 ACHIEVED DULCE NEXT

Buck spoke to the detection section of Area 51.

"Hi, General Wade here. Had any unusual readings in the last few minutes?"

"Nothing out of the ordinary, sir."

"Thank you."

Buck was a man of few words, his grin said it all. "First part done, of the flying anyway, let's hope the photo gizmos work."

Phil said, "I'm sure they will, they were made in America."

Kim smiled, "Exactly, our science is falling behind other nations because we have too much political interference, rather than let the scientists get on with it the politicians are always looking for personal advantage, offering to speed things up at the Pentagon in exchange for cash."

Phil said, "It's the same in the UK. If politicians kept their noses out of the trough medicine would make better progress. To take advantage is something taught at Eton but it's not done me any good financially but I do not have the right connections."

Buck said, "I got here on ability coming top of my class at West Point, but I'm no political soldier so I don't want any part of that rathole called the Pentagon."

Colin smiled, a rare thing for him, "I hurt people for a living so where I went to school don't matter a jot. I'll make some teas and coffees, ok?"

Meanwhile, up in the air John was on his way to his next stop which was Dulce in New Mexico. Dulce was reputed to have aliens working with American scientists and that at one time there had been a gun battle between US Special Forces and aliens. The Pentagon denied it and the affair just went on

the conspiracy net. There was a guy appeared on television to speak about it who had had his fingers cut off by a ray gun or some such. John wondered why the mission included flying over some made up story, the mission was costing a lot of tax dollars and here they were wasting some.

As he flew on at 40,000 feet he saw ahead of him several tornadoes as predicted on the TV weather. He could see them clearly and so turned south to avoid them. He then continued east and followed the Grand Canyon for a while. The craft got back on course which was just to the north of the Grand Canyon. As John did not need to manually fly the machine he had time to look at the marvels of the Grand Canyon an awe inspiring sight. It is truly one of the wonders of the natural world. [**AUTHOR'S NOTE** Only seen it on TV but it is breath taking and wholly natural]

Amazingly the air was crystal clear as the area was part of the vast American desert system which covered most of the South West and so as he flew John started to sing one of his favorite songs "I Can See For Miles" by one of his favorite bands, the Who. From the height he was he could see little human activity apart from the few roads which criss crossed the desert like some modern day Nazca lines. This made him think of how significant we seemed and yet we were capable of blowing the planet to smithereens many times over.

"Enough of this Aristotle stuff, John," he said, "concentrate, this Dulce place is just ahead."

He decelerated and gently descended to 500 feet above the Archuleta Mesa. He took a short video from above with the ground penetrating camera then moved to the edge of the mesa. He again used the ground penetration on the face of the mesa but he himself could see absolutely no activity. He finished and moved away as there were several black helicopters flying around which might have had sophisticated equipment on board which may detect him. He was not impressed with Dulce Base that

looked like an ordinary military base but had such a reputation that John believed it was extraordinary. There was a Jicarillo Apache reservation at the foot of the mesa so John pondered what did the Apache know about the affairs at the base-probably nothing. He would like to come back here on the ground and have a look round but John knew that despite his high security clearance in England he would not be permitted to return to Dulce for a look round as Americans seemed to be obsessed with secrecy. He remembered the movie *Independence Day* where the President knew nothing of Area 51 and its contents. Despite being the head of state others below him were supposed to keep things from him on the basis of "culpable deniability". If he was asked and he knew nothing about it then he could truthfully answer that he knew nothing and was free of any blame. RAF Spring Mills where John worked was supposedly a secret base but was not as most politicians knew what it was about as did the locals.

"Anyway that bit is done know for a trip to the seaside to Santa Monica Bay, playground of the rich and home of aliens which I doubt but orders is orders so onward over the mountains and desert which will be a nice scenic trip."

Back at Area 51, Buck spoke to the Pentagon and waited for them to check with Dulce Base to see if there had been any detection of the craft during its mission. It had got up close to the mesa as they knew. Buck put the communicator on speaker so they all could hear. After about 10 minutes a grizzled voice came over the loudspeaker.

"Buck, Tom Andrews here you old sidewinder. Your mission is going well, Dulce got *nada* on their detection gear so your craft is good and you got a fine pilot in Col. Thompson the dashing test pilot. Wish we had him. Anyhoo speak later, regards to Beth."

"Thanks Tom old buddy, and I do mean old, keep smiling."

Buck said to the team, "Mission done onto Mission #3 Santa Monica."...

14. #2 DONE ON TO #4

He flew in a westerly direction from Dulce to the Pacific and again, as the course was preset he had little or no need to apply his flying skills. He looked out at the desert and hills of New Mexico and Southern California.

He mused, "I would hate to crash here, I reckon you could disappear, your craft with you and never be found unless a satellite happened to be exactly above you and someone monitoring it noticed the wreckage. America is a massive country with plenty of wild areas nobody goes into. If I survived the crash I would probably only last a day without water, what a horrible way to go, I think I'd rather be killed in the crash than die of thirst. Shut up John, you miserable old wassock. Let's think about the mission. It should be an easy one as I will just be flying over the bay just looking out for para-gliders, light aircraft and helicopters but if I pilot the craft myself, I should be able to avoid any accidents. I will approach at 40,000 feet then drop down to 500 feet to take the pictures. These cameras are a marvel, if they work, so if there is an alien base below Santa Monica Bay they should bring it up clearly enough. So if it is there I wonder what the Pentagon will do? They can't nuke it as it would kill most people in Southern California with the radiation even if they use a clean bomb. Maybe they would use powerful depth charges from some of their anti-sub craft. Perhaps they will send a sub down to explore and if the aliens want to talk then they would talk. Or maybe there are no aliens and people are just imagining it, you know, someone says "Wow, did you see that?" the person next to them saw nothing but says "Yeah what do you think it was?" the first one says "An alien craft" "I think so too". The media get hold of it, the story spreads and the Pentagon make up a story that it was a weather balloon or swamp gas and so the conspiracy theories spread and fill the internet. Anyway, we are over Southern California so will soon be there, then I will fly manually just in case. Who knows I might spot some little green men."

After his soliloquy Col. Thompson flew on until he reached the coastal urban sprawl of Santa Monica with its wealth and play which of course the colonel did not begrudge as he was no communist, just a plain ordinary English socialist who never tried to put the world to rights, he still had the notion that a man's politics and religion were his own private business and not up for discussion.
He hovered over the bay and after checking all round by gently spinning in a circle he descended to 500 feet and switched on the appropriate camera which could take pictures and video through water to an incredible depth and then be able to take pictures penetrating the sea bed. He flew slowly up and down the bay whilst keeping an eye out for any craft flying to and from the coast. He must have arrived on half day closing as there was nothing in the air despite it being a beautiful summer's day.
Suddenly about 400 yards in front of him a circular craft, not unlike the one he was piloting shot up out of the water and so he stopped, hovered and used his regular camera to take a video. The craft turned towards him so he shot upwards to avoid it as it passed beneath him. Thankfully, it did nothing but fly towards the coast and disappear over the mountains.

John slowly flew towards and hovered over the place from whence the craft had surfaced and took a long video of the area switching back and forth between wide and narrow angle shots. He rose to 1500 feet to cover a wider area and continued filming. Nothing further came up out of the sea and the craft did not reappear.

"Wow, that was what you call a close encounter. Good job it didn't detect me or fire at me or I would have had to take evasive action, just like being back in Afghanistan avoiding SAMs being fired by the Taliban. I think it wasn't alien but was US military, I had better take that up with Buck as it does not want to be broadcast around if it is a secret military craft. Wonder why Santa Monica Bay though I would have thought it would be better being nearer a Pacific Coast base or even better under the

Atlantic on the East Coast, I am looking forward to seeing the video but I will not be able to tell anyone, not like the so called "top secret" work we do at RAF Spring Mills that the world and his wife know about. Buck never said anything about a naval base in the Bay so it must be assumed that what I saw was a real life, genuine USO **[AUTHOR'S NOTE** Unidentified Submerged Object an alien phenomenon that many claim to see – a good example is the Shag Harbor incident in Canada which may be found on the internet] I bet the story gets buried and we will be sworn to secrecy, not to worry Phil, Colin and me are used to being hushed up by politicians afraid to tell anyone anything. It would not be worth risking life and limb to talk to a journalist about something we have seen as they would only twist our words to suit their political agenda. Notwithstanding (great word, John) the media it will be fascinating to look at the craft closely to see if anything gives away its origin. I remember seeing the wreckage of the Roswell craft, it had the word "Video" engraved on it in English! Righty-ho up and on to Cheyenne Mountain....

15. #3 DONE ON TO #4

John turned the craft in a circle and flew over Santa Monica. No one gasped and pointed at the sky as the invisibility program still held true. John was tempted to buzz the city from a low altitude but refrained as he did not want any accident as a result of careless flying. He had a long trip of 1,112 ahead of him and again, the automatic pilot reset and set off over what was basically desert and mountains. They were beautiful to look at but a skilled pilot needs a challenge and just sitting looking out of the window was not one and so John strapped himself in to have a short nap. He slept for an hour and feeling refreshed he unstrapped, which went smoothly, and took over manual controls knowing that if he went astray the auto pilot could easily correct the course.

He kept to the preset course and tried a few wrinkles on the controls, a side slip followed by a stall, then a falling leaf and even an Immelmann turn from World War 1[**AUTHOR'S NOTE** The Immelmann turn was a combat maneuver used after an attack on another aircraft to re-position the attacking aircraft for another attack. The pilot would climb back up past the enemy aircraft and just before the stall he would apply full rudder to yaw his craft around.] All of these worked perfectly without any unnecessary vibrations or loss of control and so John turned back to the auto pilot and continued on his way. He noticed very few roads or buildings below him, this was a sparsely populated part of America. He flew on towards Colorado hoping Buck and the rest were not too bored.

*   *   *

Meanwhile, back at Area 51, the team were watching the instruments to see how John was performing.

Phil said, "Probably John has just performed a few maneuvers using manual controls, He will try to carry out one of them called an Immelmann turn, he is showing this is not just a straight flying spy

plane, it would have potential as a defensive fighter aircraft if it was fitted with guns or even as a low level attack fighter like the old Mosquito or Typhoon of World War 2. Imagine the devastation it could cause to a line of enemy tanks as it is invisible and undetectable on radar, wow! It could win a war on its own."

Colin grinned nastily. "Just think of it in our hands, MI6, we could use it for long distance assassinations taking out leaders we did not like. If we had this in World War 2 think of the enemies we could have taken out and saved millions of lives. Even just that monster Hitler would have been enough. During the Cold War we could have downed Stalin and Mao. The whole world would have been easier to live in."

There was a loud buzz on the entrance door screen. Kim went over and switched on the viewing camera. There were four large men in suits standing there.

"Hello, Doctor Poeppy, we are from the State Department here to see General Wade, these are our credentials, would you please let us in."

"Certainly," said Kim, "welcome gentlemen."

As she reached for the opening controls Colin pulled out his Glock and held it behind his back. As the State Department officials came in they all drew their MP-443 Yariginas and Colin in a blur shot all four in the forearms so they dropped their weapons.\

"Try learning English better *priyateli.*"
[**AUTHOR'S NOTE** Russian for, buddies, mates, pals et al]

"Your grammatical construction was *nevernyy*"
[**AUTHOR'S NOTE** Russian for incorrect, irregular] "The FSB should give you proper English lessons including how to speak, some of the English traitors who live in your scummy country could teach you. So then, lads, tell me why you are hear otherwise you will feel *pytka.* [**AUTHOR'S NOTE** Russian for torture]. To let you super spies

into a little secret, I work for MI6 and we know hundreds of painful ways to extract information causing the maximum amount of agony and I enjoy inflicting pain, believe you me."

The four Russian agents looked terrified as none of them thought Americans indulged in torture but of course they realized Colin came from a country with a long history of torture and imaginative styles of execution. They dreaded being hung, drawn and quartered which they had learned was the fate of traitors and spies such as William Wallace, Hugh Despenser and Guy Fawkes. The last victim of this act of barbarism was Robert Emmet in 1803 and the FSB strongly believed that MI6 would continue to use it in secret.

Colin said, "Are you here to interfere with our mission?" After he said that he took off his lab coat revealing a T-shirt he obtained online based on his favorite movie, *The Punisher,* a wonderful revenge movie showing a nice line in torture. One of the Russians recognized the T-shirt logo and said in Russian "He means business."

"I do indeed," said Colin, "all I need is a sewing kit and with skillful use of the sewing needles your screams will be heard in FSB Headquarters in the Lubyanka Building in Moscow. So, who is first."

Kim gave Colin a sewing kit used in the field and he carefully extracted a needle. He approached the leader of the troupe of spies, looked him in the eyes.

"I'll talk, please, please don't hurt me any more. You have shot me is that not enough. We were sent to take the plans for the craft you are testing as we thought there would only be scientists here not an MI6 murderer. We will go to jail pending a swap with some American agent we have taken."

Colin said, "Fine. I will not kill you..this time, but if I ever see any of the four of you in Britain I will kill you." …

16. AFTERMATH OF THE ATTACK BY THE FSB

John flew blissfully on towards Cheyenne Mountain unaware of the FSB attempted snatch of the plans for his craft. He decided that he would take manual control again at Cheyenne Mountain so he could more accurately aim the ground penetrating camera, particularly at the entrance.

Cheyenne Mountain was as secretive as Area 51. It was built in the 1960s to house NORAD which is the North American Air Defense Command, the early warning system in the event of a nuclear attack. It was supposed to have been moved to Petersen Air Base nearby but since 2015, for whatever top secret reason it had moved back inside the mountain. This was all Col. Thompson knew from the internet but he suspected it was to prevent electronic interference with the system by potential enemies of America. England did not have such a complicated and expensive system but had not suffered any missile attacks since the V1 and V2 campaigns of World war 2. John suspected his flyby would test whether America would need such a system that cost a fortune and needed constant maintenance but of course the decision was not his to make.

*   *   *

Back at Area 51 the FSB agents had been arrested by security and taken away. The team were relaxing with coffee and musing over the events.

Phil said, "I wonder how the FSB knew we were testing a new top secret aircraft. Just because the dashing test pilot turns up here means nothing, he is so famous he might just have been touring the main US bases giving lectures, which the FSB will know about if they follow him around in England."

Buck said, "The leak could be from anywhere when you think about it. It could be the Pentagon, your Ministry of Defense, your Foreign Office, our State Department or even from here as we seem to have our fair share of foreign agents working here. Colin what do you think as you are in the spying game."

Colin thought for a moment and said, "Who knows? Like us in MI6 we must keep our ears open as these spies are often careless. There was once one of the secretaries in MI5 who used to take files out with her, met a Russian contact who photographed what he needed and she then walked back into MI5 with the files and filed them away. Nobody ever challenged her and after she retired she confessed but as the matter was so embarrassing no action was taken. The same could be happening anywhere in the military or security services. Everyone has a weakness that the FSB and others can use to persuade traitors to act treacherously. The KGB used to use people's sexual preferences against them by using rent boys as bait, photograph the person then use the pictures as blackmail to get them to betray their country. With others, they get into debt and the FSB will fund them and human greed does the rest."

Kim said, "It must be difficult to find these people, especially the one you mentioned, Colin, who simply took files out unchallenged. I would imagine that is more difficult now with CCTV."

Colin replied, "You are right, Kim, some sensitive stuff is still committed to paper as computers can be hacked by nine year old kids these days, so we at MI6 do not keep personnel files or reports online. Any leads to overseas agents are kept on paper too, in fact, we could probably manage without computers."

Phil said, "I love spy films, especially English ones, you know, Bond, Smiley and all that. Often in these films the spy HQ, usually MI5 comes under attack. Has that ever happened to your place Colin?"

Colin replied, "An innocent question, or is it? I know it is innocent Phil as you are a patriotic Englishman and so I can answer it without betraying any state secrets. The answer is no, mate. If the FSB, terrorists, the Chinese or anyone tried it they would be gunned down with one kept alive to learn what we do with terrorists. We tend not to be infested with foreign agents, unlike MI5 who had

Burgess, Maclean and Philby working for them and the KGB. [**AUTHOR'S NOTE** the three people mentioned were recruited by the KGB Soviet secret service and worked at the heart of British intelligence betraying their country for material rewards. The internet has several plethoras of information about them.] They defected to Russia and good riddance. The traitors in intelligence is a theme movie makers often use but traitors within are as rare as hen's teeth so we tend not to waste our time watching each other, but if we suspect someone is betraying England we will investigate properly and if it has cost the lives of any of our agents at home or abroad they will pay dearly. I wonder, Buck, how you choose staff for here, let us say in the more sensitive areas."

Buck replied, "Human resources tends to recruit from the top universities such as MIT, where Kim here came from, but I do not know the vetting process. I presume they look at the person's home background, school work for any anti-American essays and at their social media to work out their politics. Others come from recommendations by State, by industry especially the aircraft industry and online recruitment adverts for the less sensitive areas. I will suggest to the Pentagon that there has to be a tightening up to keep the FSB and others out."

*   *   *

John had reached the area of Cheyenne Mountain and being the dashing test pilot that he was, he decided to fly into the entrance portal on the Eastern side to try to get decent pictures. It would test his flying skills to the limit and the hovering ability of the craft, but here goes....

17. A CRACKING BIT OF FLYING

John flew in a wide circle to reach the Eastern portal at 40,000 feet then slowly descended at the recommended speed of 150 miles per hour and hovered about 50 feet above the entrance road. He could see batteries of security cameras around the entrance, presumably connected to anti-aircraft weapons, probably electronic. He saw vehicles driving in and out of a wide and high entrance into the mountain. It seemed to John that secret as this place is meant to be an awful lot of people seem to know about it and/or work there. The base was on the lookout for suspicious aircraft, vehicles, incoming missiles fired accidentally or on purpose and even presumably people trying to approach the base without permission. He thought of the conspiracy theorists who tried to break in to Area 51 despite notices that trespassers would be shot, they always failed yet the Chinese and the FSB were crawling all over Area 51 due to the lax interview technique of the recruitment section of the Pentagon. John though about this and was beginning to think that maybe FSB or the Chinese secret service controlled the recruitment section at the Pentagon.

However, he had a job to do and so he went almost to the ground and flew slowly and silently into Cheyenne Mountain. He knew he could not go very far in case he was trapped, in which case the blast doors would be closed, the alarms would go off and he would be caught. Even if he was not shot but captured the mission would have failed and he would have a black mark on his record. He turned on every recording device just in case and hovered turning a complete circle. He flew very slowly out of the tunnel into the light and then after a few yards climbed to 100 feet.

He was just in time as a whole convoy of trucks roared out of the tunnel. He videoed the trucks knowing they would show the contents but in view of other things he was filming, this did not matter.

He flew up the side of the mountain filming all the way using the ground penetrating camera. He could see various gizmos poking out of the mountain. He recognized some as CCTV as seen on virtually every building in Central London, Leeds, Manchester and other major cities in England. They had cut crime in England of the major brand such as bank robberies, which, coupled with vehicle license plate recognition enabled the police to track getaway cars. The other pieces of kit he did not recognize, presumably it was some sort of radar or the like.

John only flew, he left the scientific and electronic planning to others. He looked forward to working with Joe Shaw back at RAF Spring Mills, as Joe knew lots about scientific equipment and, indeed, was always making suggestions to the scientific arm of the MoD regarding improvements to weapons and other technology. It would be like a breath of fresh air for both John and Joe to work in tandem. Joe was not afraid of flying and so on any future overseas missions Joe could accompany him.

Cheyenne Mountain is about 9,500 feet high and John flew slowly up to the summit and down the other side with the ground penetrating camera working all the time. Then for good measure he mad a quick pass over Colorado Springs. There had been no unusual cockpit sounds but that did not mean he had not been detected by the Cheyenne Mountain base defensive equipment. He remembered he would not be shot down but if he had been detected Gen. Wade would be informed as would be the Pentagon.

Suddenly, just before he reached the portal on the Western side of the mountain three helicopters appeared and John just avoided colliding with them. They flew off towards the West without seeming to have noticed him but again, these were personnel transport which carried no armament who would radio in if he had been seen. Kim would communicate with him by the watch if he had been spotted which would terminate the mission early and maybe he and his buddies would not be paid. As nothing

had happened watch wise he turned East heading in the direction of Hangar 18 of Wright Patterson Airbase in Ohio to film the hangar looking for old alien craft. He knew Wright Patterson had a large intelligence contingent based there and so there must be something worth hiding and as it may be kept underground he decided to use his initiative and film the rest of the base with the ground penetrating camera just to be thorough.

It was a long trip of 1,200 miles plus but with the automatic preprogrammed equipment on board he could again sleep for a quick half hour before he arrived there. He decided on manual flying at 75 feet as that would clear most buildings and of course he would need to be alert for aircraft and helicopters taking off and landing, especially those that could take off vertically.

*   *   *

Back at Area 51, Gen. Wade rang the commander at Santa Monica Naval Air Station and the commander at Dulce. Both checked with the radar and other electronic defense operatives. Dulce came up negative, but the commander, Co. DeSean Jackson had something interesting to say.

"Hello Gen. Wade our sensors picked up a craft surfacing fro beneath the sea. About a dozen of our men picked it up on visual. It was one of those pesky USOs we see from time to time. I hope your guy got a good video of it so we can maybe identify the country of origin. If a foreign power has a base in Santa Monica Bay we need to take it out as a matter of national security, so please keep us in the loop. Over and out."…

18. #4 DONE ON TO THE LAST ONE

Phil said, "The Santa Monica base are sure it was not John they picked up, aren't they?"

Buck replied, "They have some of the best detection equipment outside Cheyenne Mountain and so it was not John that they got but some kind of USO." [**AUTHOR'S NOTE** USOs are Unidentified Submerged Objects they can be anything from static rock formations, to enemy submarines to giant marine animals (Megalodon anyone?). The Santa Monica anomaly has featured in many television documentaries about conspiracy theories suggesting it is an alien base] It is believed by many conspiracy theories that there is an underwater alien base in Santa Monica Bay as there have been hundreds of sightings over the years of flying discs. What do you guys think?"

Colin said, "A Russian or Chinese submarine base that sends up drones to spy out the Pacific coast. These drones are quick and also it is US policy not to fly missiles over American soil so the navy never try to shoot them down."

Kim continued, "I agree with Colin, there are no aliens there, if indeed there are any anywhere. What I cannot see though is how the Russians or Chinese could get the base built. Even if it was a natural formation like a vast cave it would be impossible to bring in thousands of tons of equipment undetected. Also, that area of Santa Monica Bay about six miles offshore is very deep, about 2,000 feet beyond the range of divers plus there are no ROVs capable of assembling complex machinery."

Phil said, " I watch conspiracy documentaries mainly for the laugh, but they make interesting points about portals, which are sort of gateways like in the movie *Stargate,* a way to get from A to B almost instantly. Some guy said Bigfoot travels by portals across America which is why it is seen in so many different places and it is connected to UFO sightings."

Buck said, "We are drifting into unknown waters here. I think it is someone's naval base, probably ours that sends up drones to check security of the military bases on the Pacific coast and maybe checks China and Siberia too. It is pointless to speculate but the Pentagon would willingly put out UFO stories to keep the public from thinking about the real purpose of the base. It still leaves the mystery of how it got there but that is nothing to us other than normal human curiosity."

*   *   *

John was flying on automatic pilot heading for Wright Patterson base in Ohio. Personally he did not think there would be much that was secret there, particularly anything alien in origin such as the Roswell Crash debris or the craft that crashed in Kecksburg, Pennsylvania both well over fifty years ago. No, he felt that anything that had to be top secret would be kept underground in secure facilities. He had read about the thousands of miles of tunnels beneath Denver Airport, one of which was supposed to connect to Area 51. In fact, he had watched a whole series of programs on BBC2 about the miles of tunnels under major cities whose purpose was not always apparent but made for interesting speculation, especially the ones under Washington DC and Moscow. He was confident that the ground penetrating radar could give an accurate picture of what was down there and this would enable the Pentagon to beef up its security as both Russia and China had ground penetrating kit which had trickled down to the police and even to the lads at *Time Team.*

He ceased his random thinking as he arrived in front of Wright Patterson, which had a personnel force of 30,000 and was the biggest employer in Ohio. Anything secret known about by 30,000 people is not really a secret, hence the underground thinking. He switched to manual flying at 100 feet which was quite hazardous but he wanted to get the best detailed shots possible. He switched on every camera

on board and flew slowly over the base taking images of every building and the runways in case of underground facilities. He noticed an anomaly, parked on the runway nearest to the main office complex was *Air Force One*, the President's plane. Maybe he was just visiting on a glad handing mission or perhaps the aircraft was there for a service or for new equipment to be fitted. The aircraft was normally kept at Andrews Air Base in Maryland but it was used to ferry the president from A to B. If the conspiracy nuts saw it they would be imagining the president was there to meet aliens or inspect the Roswell stuff. However, he had completed his inspection and took the craft up to 50,000 feet and switched to auto pilot which would take him back to Area 51 and a nice meal, shower and a bit of kip.

[**AUTHOR'S NOTE** All the information about Wright Patterson etc was gleaned from a brief search of the internet. Some of it is conspiracy so may not be true, but I write fiction so I can put what I want. I am not a spook with access to top secret stuff, or am I…]

*   *   *

The scene shifts back to Area 51 and the four are drinking yet another coffee. Kim and Phil checked John's timetable and said that he should be on his way home.

Buck spoke to his contacts at Cheyenne Mountain and also Wright Patterson. After a wait of a couple of minutes both communicated back to Buck with confirmation that there was nothing weird on their detection equipment nor had anyone reported any visual sightings especially as the president was visiting Wright Patterson just to say "Howdy Do."

Colin said, "Job's a good 'un. When he gets back we can be shocked by the pretty pictures or bored out of our heads." …

19. OH NO!!

John was happily relaxing with the auto pilot on drinking the last of his water flask but knowing that he would be home in an hour or so. He passed the time by singing a few of his favorite songs from his childhood and thinking of how Leeds Rhinos would perform for the rest of the season. He was due some leave and so he fancied going back to Leeds and taking in a couple of Rhino's games and maybe a three day match of Yorkshire cricket in the County Championship. He was a celeb and so he would need a bit of a disguise other than shades which were a bit too obvious, especially at a Rhino's match. This led him to remember the Rhinos achievements over the last few years especially winning the treble. Due to flying commitments he could not attend too many matches due to the kidnap risk which was ever present but he thought if it happened and he yelled for help the Rhinos fans would have sprung into action.

These thoughts passed the time on the journey home. Suddenly, he felt a loss of power. The engine was quiet anyway but this loss of power went from worrying to full scale disaster mode. He plugged in the safety straps which were designed to hold the body tightly and securely in the event of a crash. His body would not be slammed into the control console on impact and so he knew if he could make any sort of landing he would survive. He was at 40,000 feet descending rapidly and he needed to try to glide the machine down, hopefully without wrecking the cameras and other equipment on board.

He switched to manual control, this worked, and began to gently slip from side to side in a falling leaf descent much like pilots had done in World War II when their engines had stopped. He knew he was over the Nevada desert and so reckoned on landing in a soft patch of sand if he could come down gently. He decelerated gently but was still going at a fair old lick when he hit the ground. He bounced

several times before coming to a halt at the foot of a huge mountain of sand somewhere in the Nevada Desert.

John knew nothing of this as the initial impact jerked his neck back causing blissful unconsciousness. The bouncing along, up and down had put strains on every joint in his body and so he remained unconscious for the rest of the day and the night too.

The craft remained cloaked and damage to the craft was minimal, which is more than could be said for the pilot.

*   *   *

Back at Area 51, time passed slowly. Every fifteen minutes a member of the quartet would try to raise John on his watch which functioned as a radio transmitter/receiver on a private band. It was not a computer, nor did it have the capability of controlling the craft. It was a sound only device.

They simply said, "John, if you can hear us please reply and we will try to get you out of there." There was not much sleep that night as all four were worried sick about John's fate, they did not give a fig for the craft, it was clearly a working failure despite having had the most thorough of checks throughout both at the manufacturers and at Area 51 too.

They went to breakfast in the canteen keeping conversation to a minimum and avoiding contact with other people in there.

When they returned to their hangar the mood was sombre. Only Phil remained optimistic.

"John is the best pilot ever so I think he made a landing somewhere safely and maybe is catching up on some sleep. We have been told it is a reliable craft and very sturdy. John can fly anything, I remember seeing him at Elvington Air Show once flying a replica of the Bleriot plane that first crossed the Channel in 1909 and doing all kinds of aerobatics in it, flinging it across the sky every which way. He is OK, this I believe." [**AUTHOR'S NOTE** Elvington Airfield near York puts on an annual air show featuring Spitfires, Wellingtons and other goodies but probably not a Bleriot replica, but it is a good image, innit?]

Colin gave Phil a manly hug which scared Phil.

Colin said, "You are right Phil, mate. John is not called the Dashing Test Pilot for nothing and he vowed to be at the game on Sunday to watch Essex win the County Championship. I'm sure he will be there with us, not in spirit but in body, he is one tough guy and one of the most resourceful people on earth. Let's keep our hopes beaming like a lighthouse light and let's find him."

These two speeches plus a couple of cups of strong coffee stiffened the resolve of the crew. They decided to only make the call to John every 30 minutes but make the call last a few minutes. Colin suggested they mention things John liked such as Cricket, the

Leeds Rhinos, the river at Otley and 1970s rock music.

Colin went first reeling off a string of great players from both the Rhinos and Yorkshire. Next was Phil's turn, he looked up Otley on the internet and began to describe the lovely Wharfmeadows Park on the River Wharf [**AUTHOR'S NOTE** I lived in Otley for over 40 years and thought it worthy of a plug]. Kim was next and she was comparing American and British rock bands of the 70s using a few websites she found. Then it was Buck Wade's go at contacting John, he chose American Presidents and starting at George Washington he began to slowly recite there names, He had reached William Howard Taft when...

20. GETTING JOHN OUT OF HIS SEAT

The guys in Area 51 were now genuinely worried for John, they continued trying his watch radio every fifteen minutes but without any success.

Phil said dolefully, "He is lost out in the desert and will never be found. That accursed craft will remain invisible for ever as it is light powered and there is nobody who can turn the cloaking device off. I can see why cowardly American pilots turned down the gig. It was a suicide mission."

Colin looked grimly at Phil. "Pull yourself together man. John is resourceful as well as dashing, he will get back to us."

Kim had just finished her turn on the radio and said, "Nothing, no response not even static."

Buck said, "We will just keep trying, that is all we can do."

*   *   *

John had been unconscious for hours strapped into his seat. He did not know it but the crash landing had strained every joint, bone, muscle, cartilage and sinew in his body but amazingly nothing was broken. Also, he had no cuts or tears only the immense strains, the shock of which rendered him unconscious. He was slowly coming round to a wall of pain which made him yell out.

This yell operated his watch radio so that the guys in Area 51 heard him.

Buck rushed to the communication screen and said in as calm a voice as possible, "John you are alive."

John replied, "Very much so but I am in one huge mess of pain. The landing slammed me into the harness and I appear to have strained every part of my body except my hair. I do not have a quick release so I am stuck in the harness being roasted alive. Get me out of here!"

Kim had the screen up showing the pilot's seat and saw at the frontof each armrest was a red protrusion labeled "Emergency release to be used if console release damaged."

She said loudly, "John on the left armrest first of all there is a small red protrusion, press this and it should start to release you."

John replied, "The restraint round my throat is very tight so I will try anything once."

He extended his left little finger and pressed. His little finger was released which he passed on to the guys.

"Again, John," came the chorus.

This time the ring finger on his left hand released. Next press the middle finger and the next his left index finger, finally his thumb was released.

He said, "All my left hand fingers are free so I will keep going."

In quick succession he released his left wrist, his left forearm, his left elbow, his left bicep and his left shoulder.

Kim said stop, "What was the last thing you released?"

John replied, "My left shoulder, why?"

Kim said, "Reach for the red protrusion on the right armrest now and repeat the entire process stopping when you have released your right shoulder."

John did just so releasing, on his right side all his fingers and thumb, wrist, forearm, elbow, bicep and shoulder.

"All done," he said.

"Now go back to the left protrusion slowly pressing it so each press it will release a piece of the strapping down to your waist. John did this and at the first press it released the band around his

head which was a great weight off his mind. [**AUTHOR'S NOTE** Well I thought it was funny, start the car]. The next press released the tight band around his throat which was a massive relief as he could breathe freely again. The next released his chest, then his stomach and then his waist. He reported his progress back to Kim.

Kim said, "Finish on the right protrusion until you are free, John."

John pressed the right protrusion which freed both thighs simultaneously. The next press freed both knees then followed both shins, both ankles and finally both feet.

John said, "Free at last bit I am in excruciating pain, everything has been strained in the crash. I will need a chiropractor when I get back, if I get back."

Colin said, "You will mate. This cloaking thing makes it impossible for us to come to you, you will have to come to us. Look out of the front screen and describe what you see."

"I am at the foot of a huge hill that just goes onward and upwards but looks climbable even in my present state of play."

Kim used a very sophisticated tool to find where John could be. One area stood out which she showed to the others.

She said, "John, the hill is four miles from where you are to the summit, there is then a further three miles of flat land, then a downward slope of two miles and finally an artificial forest of one mile will bring you to one of our outposts where we can meet you. If we set off to find you we will probably not find you so we will wait for you."

Buck said, "There are two satellites cross this area evry thirty minutes each as they are on a circular controlled orbit just of the area around us, one is Russian and one Chinese. This means you will have to ditch the NASA suit. Have you any other clothes you can wear?"

John replied, "My chinos I have on under my flying suit and I am wearing desert boots but no top, so I will get a mass suntan."

Buck said, "We can deal with that when we get you back. You need to walk ten miles in really hot weather with multiple injuries and wearing no top. Can you do it, buddy?"

"I'm not called the dashing test pilot for nothing I will do this. Please have water available at the post as I will have a rather large thirst when I get there."...

21. JOHN CROSSES THE DESERT

John moved gingerly around the cabin of the craft. The pain was intense but tolerable and so he knew he would be able to make it if he kept going, to stop for a rest could cause problems. He opened the door to the craft and looked out, basically it was hot and dry, he might get sunstroke, die of thirst, fall over and not be able to get back up, be eaten by a dragon or hit by an asteroid but apart from that his internal fortitude would get him through. For the last ten years he had taken part in at least one marathon a year and every other year he had participated in the Three Peaks Race in Yorkshire scrambling up and down three mountains in the North Pennines, so he knew he could get the distance and could take the pain.

Phil's voice came over the radio. "John, I suggest you run the whole way if you can and I suggest for the uphill section you try to run like Steve Cram by taking giant strides and pushing off hard each stride. If your stride is nine feet you will cover the distance three times as quick."

John replied with a croaky voice as the strapping had done some damage to his throat, "Good thinking, Phil I will do that."

Buck chipped in with, "We will tell you when each of the two satellites are in your area. Just stand still and put your hands on your head. The lack of movement and the fact that you are not wearing bright reflective clothing will make you undetectable. Keep in touch if you can and we will meet you at the outpost, it is connected by an underground tunnel to our base and we have a little subway train we can use."

Kim said, "We will have doctors here to sort you out. Oh, if you come across any dangerous animals, such as snakes, we can make the radio give off a high frequency sound that will scare them off, all being well."

Colin spoke finally, "Good luck, mate. When you are back we will go pick up the craft and watch the pictures of the aliens with you. Also, we will look into why it crashed. I think sabotage and so I will find out from the FSB scum we are holding who did it, when I get going with my several hundred ingenious tortures nobody lasts very long."

John climbed out of the craft and locked it with the credit card, the cloaking device was still on. He felt a square shape in the knee pocket of his chinos. He reached into the pocket and saw it was his pager, an old fashioned device that still worked, he hoped. He placed it in one of the air intakes out of the sun and hoped they would be able to use it to find the craft again. He had a good look round and memorized the salient features in the area then set out on his run uphill for four miles. He took Phil's advice and pushed off each time achieving a stride length of nine feet.

He refrained from looking at his watch as the time was unimportant, he just kept his ears open for anything coming in fro the guys.

He was making good time when he heard Buck say, "Satellite stand still."

He stood still and put his hands on his head. After about twenty seconds Buck said that it was in order to move once more.

The fact that he had been unconscious for so long meant that amazingly he did not feel tired and so he

made good time running up the hill with half hourly pauses for the satellites passing over head.
Eventually he reached the top of the hill and told the team so.

Kim said, "Well done, John. Now keep going on the flat for three miles, we think we know where you are if there is a single pyramid shaped peak in the distance run towards that."

John croaked, "I see it Kim I will get to the end I have done the hardest part."

He was very thirsty but he pushed that out of his mind as he also did the pain he was in from every joint. He was determined to survive and see those pictures he had taken. He ran on the flat which after a while eased his screaming thigh muscles and soon reached the beginning of the downhill two mile stretch. He knew from his fell races not to go too quickly as downhill running could cause the calf muscles to seize up so he did it steadily.

He could barely speak now because his tongue had swollen due to thirst. He told the guys he was on the downhill section and could see the forest in the distance.

Buck said, "The forest is artificial so we can light your way through it but can't come out to meet you due to those satellites but there is a concealed elevator that will bring you down to the post."

John "copied that" and ran the downhill stretch in record time, if there had been a record for that stretch of desert.

He reached the forest and Buck said, "The watch will trigger arrows which will light up in green for five seconds, just follow the arrows which will bring you to a large cactus, Tell us when you are there so we can give you instructions about operating it. Oh, by the way, while going through the forest, which is cloaked from the satellites you have to sing *Yellow Brick Road* from *The Wizard of Oz.* We are heading underground and will meet you at the post."

*   *   *

Kim and the others went down to the tunnels which had an entrance in what looked like a tool shed outside their hangar. A small electric cart took them the fifteen miles to the outpost by simply punching in the numbers. …

22. OUTPOST

John moved slowly through the trees of the artificial forest keeping his eyes focused to the ground so he could see the arrows as they were lit up by the watch. The sun had caused his eyes to feel very sore but he refrained from rubbing them as that would make them worse. He thought about various things he would need when they got back to Area 51. He needed water quite quickly followed by coffee. He needed all his joints adjusting by a chiropractor, some sort of eye treatment for his sore eyes, lip balm, a cooling lotion for the damage to his skin, but above all he was desperate to see what he had filmed.

He said into his watch, "I am in the forest following the arrows."

Kim replied, "Let us know when you are through as we do not want you at the cactus when a satellite is overhead. This cactus is top secret."

"Copy that."

"We are at the outpost and so we will have to get you back to our hangar for treatment as soon as possible."

"Copy that also."

Although he knew the forest was artificial he was still a bit concerned about wildlife as most things that lived in the desert had to be poisonous to immobilize their prey to prevent it running off. Also, he started thinking about giant ants and spiders from the 1950s creature features that had been rendered large by fallout from the atomic bomb tests in the desert. He had enjoyed *Them!* With the giant ants ending up in the storm drains of Los Angeles, but that was fiction- - -or was it? He thought he would ask anyway.

Kim replied to his question, "There could be some small rodents and maybe a few snakes but giant ants are unlikely as they have exoskeletons which would be unable to sustain their weight as they have skinny legs and also they would not be able to take in enough oxygen as they breathe through holes in their skin called traches instead of lungs. The radio is sending out a high pitched sound above human hearing that should keep snakes away as they mainly avoid confrontation unless they are threatened. We do not think the satellites of the Russians or Chinese could pick up the sound and in any event there is nothing to see."

John continued his walk through the fake forest glad to have a bit of shade from the unrelenting sun and also being grateful that he had not fallen over. Eventually he reached the edge of the forest after about a mile and reported in.

Kim said, "Go to the large lonely cactus now, you still have fifteen minutes, grasp the right hand branch and pull it towards you. Then the left hand branch and push it away from you."

John complied. There was a rumbling sound and a tall rectangular structure appeared from beneath the sand. It was an elevator known as a lift in England. John got in and it shot downwards roughly fifty feet. The doors opened and John exited to be welcomed by Buck, Kim, Phil and Colin. None of them patted him on the back as it looked very sore indeed.

The technician at the outpost was Corporal Jones from Poughkeepsie. He gave John a tumbler of ice cold water which John sipped appreciatively. His swollen tongue shrank so he was able to speak.

"I need my sunburn seeing to and my joints adjusted soon, if we could go soon please."

Buck said, "We will go now. Thank you Cpl Jones for keeping us entertained with your videos of concerts by *Against The Current,* also from Poughkeepsie, a very fine rock band." **[AUTHOR'S**

NOTE Bit of self-indulgence here as *Against The Current* are one of my favorite bands. Do check them out on YouTube].

After another swig of water John was good to go. They mounted the electric carriage. John winced as his raw back touched the seat and he had pain in most joints from the change of position from standing and walking to sitting. Colin drove the vehicle swiftly as all these electric carriages were designed to avoid the bumping and jerking that subway carriages usually had.

Buck said, "When we get back two doctors will be able to see you. I texted them to be prepared with sun lotion, lip balm and chiropractic skills. When you have had your treatment we will let Colin do his thing with one unlucky gent from the FSB and we will then eat. After that we will go to the movies to see some science fact and maybe see things we will never unsee. The craft will be fine until tomorrow where it is. Just us will pick it up but we will think about that tomorrow. Meanwhile off we jolly well go as you English say."

"No we don't, except at Eton." said Phil grinning happily now he had redeemed himself after his poor performance back at RAF Spring Mills.

John was happy to have got through his hike in one piece and was actually looking forward to being manipulated by a chiropractor.

They arrived back at the hangar to be greeted by the two doctors, Dr Foster who would treat the sunburn first and Dr Chung who was a qualified chiropractor as well as a surgeon.

Dr Foster applied lip balm quickly which soaked in and relieved the cracking of John's lips.

He then generously smeared John's upper body and head with a cream that was instantly absorbed, then after a minute John steamed as the heat left him.

Dr Chung took over and gently manipulated every joint in John's body accompanied by cracks and crunches from everywhere especially a giant crack from John's neck which caused John to sigh in relief.

After the doctors had gone they all had coffee. John put on a clean t shirt and jeans and they set off for the canteen, a happy bunch looking forward to seeing the videos, which they had electronically transferred from the craft to the computers in their hangar. …

23. THE VIDEOS AND POOR FSB MAN

Buck rang security to ask them to bring Podnin to them. After a few minutes Podnin was brought in with his arm in a cast after Colin's harsh treatment of it. Podnin was made to sit down facing our heroes and his guards were told by Phil to go for a cuppa and a bun in the canteen to be charged to Buck. The guards smiled and one said for them to text the guards when they were done.

The guards left for their tea break and Buck looked at Podnin and said, "Colin here wants a word with you, you have been a bad boy."

Podnin looked terrified as Colin had a chisel in one hand and a hammer in the other.

He gave Podnin a look of such hatred that Podnin shrank back in his seat.

"Podnin, you *grayaznaya svinya.* [**AUTHOR'S NOTE** Russian for filthy pig] Before you were recruited by the FSB you were a flight engineer with the Russian air force and when with the FSB your understanding would be useful in sabotaging craft. Am I correct?" Podnin nodded dolefully.

Colin said, "I want you to tell my general what you did to the craft, in English, so we can fix it. I will be delighted if you do not wish to say anything, for which you have the right but I will be forced to use my rather rusty medical skills with these precision implements to amputate both legs and both arms. Normally I would use a general anesthetic but you FSB guys are taught to tolerate pain. Let's see if you can remain silent as I operate."

Podnin screamed, "NO! PLEASE NO! I will talk. General please keep that madman away from me, I will tell you what I did and you can fix it instantly."

Colin laughed maniacally which sent a chill through everyone.

John said, "I'm glad you're on our side, big lad."

Podnin explained what he had done and Kim did the necessary repairs which were quite simple while Phil put them into the report which would go to the Pentagon.

Buck texted the guards to return when their break was over and said to Podnin, "Due to your cooperation and the severe injuries inflicted on you we will fly you to the Pentagon with instructions to exchange you for an agent of ours that you guys are holding."

Buck explained this proposal to the guards who promised to get it done and took Podnin away.

Kim set up the link to the large monitor screen so they could watch the films John had taken, assuming the video equipment worked.

The first film they watched was of Hangar 7 just up the base. The film was to look for any traces of alien craft from Roswell in 1947. It lasted about three minutes and merely showed an empty hangar. Phil pointed out what looked like scorch marks on the concrete floor but they could be recent.

Kim said, "I never expected there to be anything but at least the video equipment works."

The next film of about twelve minutes duration was of Dulce Base. Again, no aliens were visible but there were many technicians in hazmat suits carrying precision instruments whose use the team did not know.

Buck said, "I think it is a base for military hardware development, maybe craft like you flew,

John, which for all intents and purposes look like UFOs."

John replied, "I agree, Buck."

Then they hit the jackpot. Santa Monica Bay. John had filmed a UFO leaving an opening in the sea bed and then cloaking just before it reached the surface.

Phil said with glee, "A real flying saucer, not one of ours, not Russian or Chinese but a definite alien, how terrifically spiffing."

Buck smiled, "I agree Phil the X Files is true, aliens are on the earth. However, we must keep this juicy secret to ourselves and leave it to the Pentagon to muddy the waters to avoid the people of California panicking like they did in 1941. That one back then could have come from Santa Monica Bay."
[**AUTHOR'S NOTE** see Battle of Los Angeles on Wikipedia- it is such a strange happening when ack-ack shells were bouncing off a disc shaped craft—no weather balloon or swamp gas was this little beauty it was alien.]

After that assignment they moved on to Cheyenne Mountain and here all five agreed the defenses needed bolstering up with some form of motion detectors that could detect a cloaked craft although not even Kim could think of a way it could be done but the military would come up with a solution.

Finally they looked at a short film of Hangar 15 at Wright-Patterson Air Force Base just east of Dayton, Ohio.

The hangar was vast with much equipment they all recognized but nothing out of the ordinary. Suddenly, Kim cried out, "There, in that corner in that box, can you see it? It is a box covered by a thick layer of concrete lined with lead but look what's in it."

She zoomed in to the box. In it was the classic alien body. It had large eyes, a bald head, no nose and a small opening where a mouth should be. The body was egg shaped and thin and the arms and legs were like elastic bands.

Colin said, "I once saw a photo of one that had crashed on Dartmoor but had died. We burned it and buried the ashes and the story before the media got hold of it. It looked like this one for sure."

Buck said, "The Pentagon will have to find a better place than that to keep alien bodies but I think we agree aliens exist. Now I think we should eat, sleep and sort out the paperwork tomorrow." …

24. CANTEEN TALK

The team were enjoying a hearty meal of ham salad and chatting about random things not connected to the mission when Colin looked deep in thought.

Phil said, "Penny for them, Colin, you look worried sir."

Colin replied, "I do not think we got all the FSB agents and so I am just going to do some electronics with my boss. There, that's it. In less than thirty seconds it will show us if there are any of their agents we have missed."

Colin's phone began to play *Breaking The Law* by Judas Priest and showed three red dots on a floor plan of the canteen.

Colin said, "Walk nonchalantly to the back right as if we are going to the loos. There are three of them on the corner table. Let's get them."

The team were all smiles and relaxed as they headed for the bathrooms. As they neared them they turned swiftly. Buck and Kim grabbed one man, John and Phil another and Colin got the biggest in a ferocious headlock.

The large FSB agent recognized Colin and told his companions not to resist. Buck called the guards who were quite getting used to it and again Buck phoned the Pentagon to explain.

The man at the Pentagon said, "Heads will roll for someone employing FSB agents in the US defense industry."

Buck replied, "All it takes is to get the CIA and England's MI6 to liaise with you, they have sensational identity software that could pick out agents. You could even arrest them on the day they start but we do need to keep the country safe."

The low loader was ready to go and they all got on board. Buck spoke to the main gate and asked for all inward traffic to be held for about twenty minutes and he gave the same message to the men on the exit gate from the base buildings.

Colin input John's pager number and a map appeared giving the location of the craft. It was five miles down the road then twenty miles into the desert but well away from any of the Area 51 runways. They set off and once they were out of the compound Colin switched on the cloaking device. He drove the low loader extremely quickly so that after a few minutes they turned off into the desert.

Colin said, "I looked up the specs for this beauty and it is all terrain, it could drive right up Mount Everest so this bit of sand and rocks will be easy but I will take it steadily. If you had come out on this route John I don't think you would have made it."

Colin drove on. It was a remarkably smooth ride so they were able to talk.

Phil said to Kim, "John had switched the craft off apart from the cloaking device, so how were you able to access the films?"

Kim replied, "We have developed a top secret piece of kit that bypasses the controls and accesses all records, it could put spies out of business."

Colin said, "Nothing lasts forever, the other side will invent something to counteract it. There will always be a need for field agents."

They reached the location of the craft.

Buck said, "The Chinese satellite will be overhead in a minute so let us just wait five minutes then we will attach the grabs. When the Russian craft has gone we can haul it aboard and cloak everything."

This they did, then John inserted the credit card, opened the hatch, got in and uncloaked the craft. Colin moved the vehicle in front of the craft and moved the magnetic grabs to where they were needed.

The rest of the team moved the four grabs into position and the magnetic force did the rest.
[**AUTHOR'S NOTE** these grabs are fictional please bear that in mind as this is not a scientific text book.] John then cloaked the craft, they all got back into the cab of the low loader which Colin cloaked and they waited.

Once Buck gave the all clear John went back to to the craft and switched off the cloaking device. Colin hauled the craft aboard the low loader, then John switched on the cloaking device once more.
They were all now back in the cab so Colin cloaked the low loader. This whole operation had taken a while so they waited for the next satellite to pass over before they set off. Colin drove more modestly to avoid becoming stuck in the sand with the extra weight and it was uneventful. It took them just over an hour to reach the road.

Buck again rang the main gate and the exit gate as before. There was no traffic on the roads but to make sure, Buck had traffic held up for thirty minutes but they made it back well within that time. Once at the gate of their hangar Buck opened the gate, Colin drove through it and into the hangar perfectly. They then disembarked and made the low loader and the craft visible.

Buck reported to the Pentagon that the craft was fine and could be collected for onward transportation to parts unknown.

"Well that's a job well done," said Phil, "life will be a bit dull after this going back to being a travel clerk with the FO. [**AUTHOR'S NOTE** Foreign and Commonwealth Office headed up at the time the story is set by Boris Johnson].

John said, "I will take some leave to watch cricket then go back to test piloting."

Colin said, "I am part of an ongoing investigation into certain members of certain government departments who are passing our secrets on to certain foreign agents who are in turn selling them to certain foreign governments."

Buck said, "I think we all need a good nights rest then we will get you on the London flight from Vegas. It has been a great adventure, especially for you John, The dashing test pilot."…

25. BACK TO JOLLY OLD ENGLAND

Goodbyes were said and Buck took the guys to the Jane flight to Vegas. They were less than an hour in McCarron airport before they boarded for London. Phil texted Charlotte Pinkney-Brabazon with their time of arrival so that a car could pick them up.

The flight to London was also uneventful. As on their outward journey the conversation was light and ordinary in case of eavesdroppers. They settled down to a long flight with the occasional nap. Their choice of viewing was quite broad. John watched some concerts by *Against The Current* as the lads had been raving about them. Phil watched some Leeds Rhinos matches as he had made it his determination to watch some rugby league live as there were two teams in the London area, London Broncos and London Skolars so he thought he would give it a whirl. Colin watched several historical documentaries on the Tudors due to his penchant for torture but at heart he was a gentle man, he only dealt harshly with enemies of the country.

When they arrived at Heathrow they were met by the fragrant Charlotte Pinkney-Brabazon who had been given Boris's permission to use one of the Foreign Office limousines normally reserved for visiting foreign dignitaries. They were whisked back to the FO in style.

When they arrived back at the Foreign Office they were ushered into Boris's plush office. Also there to greet them was Philip Hammond, the Defense Secretary who looked very pleased.

Boris said, "Well done, gentlemen. Gen Wade told me your mission had been more than successful as you not only tested the craft and its equipment but you also caught a nest of agents of a foreign power.

The Prime Minister is delighted with you but as this was a secret mission, medals are not permitted to be issued, but I am sure you do not mind."

Colin said, "We were only doing our duty and we got the job done so we will be satisfied with that and we will be paid by the Americans."

Philip Hammond said, "That has already been done, it is in your bank account and will be tax free, you will be glad to know."

Boris said, "I believe you took some interesting films of certain sensitive areas. Do you wish to share this information with us."

John said, "Sorry, sirs, but the Americans made us sign away that right so I am very sorry but we are not allowed to. You gentlemen know how that works, I am sure."

Boris smiled and said, "We understand perfectly. Everything is a secret these days so that the public do not panic and I think that is a good thing. The internet will tend to guess about things but as this mission has been done on the quiet I do not think there will be much discussion except by the conspiracy theorists."

John continued, "Nothing really to discuss it was quite routine really."

Boris said, "Looking to the future now. John you will continue to be based at RAF Spring Mills as the legend that is the Dashing Test Pilot. Is that what you want to do, from now on assisted by Sgt Joe Shaw who has been promoted and had a nice backdated pay rise from Mr Hammond?"

John replied, "Indeed it is, thank you."

Boris went on, "Phil, you have distinguished yourself on this mission, doing things beyond the call of duty and therefore, Philip Hammond and myself have decided to transfer you to the MoD to head up an information gathering section which will liaise with the security services to see if we can reduce the number of hostile spies in our country. It will mean a pay rise but will be a leg up the ladder as well. Is that in order as you are wasted as a travel clerk."

Phil replied, "Thank you sirs, I would be honored to serve in this new capacity."

Philip Hammond said to Colin, "We are in your debt and need you to continue in your present job for the sake of your country, with a pay rise of course. Can you tell us your real name please?"

Colin said, "I thank you gentlemen and will continue to work for my country to the best of my ability. My real name? If I told you it I would have to kill you, which would be an act of treason, so no you will never know. I have not had a holiday for years and would appreciate a fortnight off."

Philip said, "I knew you would ask for that and so to facilitate that here is a credit card you can use, spend as much as you like."

"Thank you very much, as I have no vices it will not cost much."

Boris pressed the intercom.

"Charlotte, can you come in please."

The delectable Charlotte Pinkney-Brabazon swept in, looked at Phil Jackson and said "Will you go out with me Phil, please."

Phil looked staggered. 'You want to go out with m-me? I am so unworthy."

Boris said, "You are a hero, you deserve a beautiful lady."

Phil said, "I would be delighted."

*   *   *

So ends the first adventure of the Dashing Test Pilot. Will there be more? Maybe.